I0575399

CONUNDRUM

AN INVASION UNIVERSE STORY

JOHNNY B. TRUANT

STERLING & STONE

CONUNDRUM

1

THE NOISE.

The small noise, intruding on Nicole's spinning consciousness — perhaps a set of manicured nails, tapping singly on Formica.

Marble made a sound that spoke of solidity. The kind of material you could beat up, could trust. This sound was cheaper. A discount pen tapping against wood paneling. A stylus with rattling insides, thrummed on a tablet with its screen already shattered.

It wasn't the kind of sound Nicole abided. Out of place, here in the world she'd clawed her way to the top of.

Except, when she lifted her aching head, she found herself far from her Manhattan flat.

Nicole wasn't in bed, on a couch, or even in a chair. She was on the floor, stomach-down, head to one side. Something viscous lubricated her smallest movements — saliva, maybe blood.

She didn't lay on beautiful hardwood or imported tile. Wasn't even in Mike's studio, where she'd paid extra to skim the floors in concrete. He lived in a top-end building, stone between each unit so you wouldn't hear it if Grandma next door fell asleep with her hearing aid off and her juke cranked to crazy. The idea that she'd had to pay more to leave the concrete showing was, in a word, ludicrous.

As she blinked toward consciousness and saw the floor beneath her — cool metal, more daring than even she'd have in her kitchen — some lizard part of her mind told Nicole to hold her tongue, to throttle her sarcasm even if it promised to confine itself to her thoughts.

Who floored in aluminum? Or steel? Or iron? As a design choice, it stunk. As the reality before her, it was terrifying.

For a few seconds she stayed frozen.

Am I on the floor at home?

Explain the metal if you are.

Did I faint in public? Home Depot, perhaps, while picking out roofing?

If so, where's the public?

She still hadn't lifted her head. Didn't trust that yet. From her vantage point, she took in more metal at eye level, then metallic claws ahead — a bed, or something to sit on, framed in hard silver edges. But no public, no people.

Nobody was there.

Come on, girl. Sit up. Just look around, nice and easy.

But her heart hammered. She'd gotten back enough blood to know this wasn't right, that puzzle pieces weren't fitting together.

Nicole Davies didn't back down. She was a woman who always faced what was in front of her.

She wiped a finger between her lip and the floor. Clear and wet. Saliva, but no blood. Nothing hurt. So she hadn't been assaulted. At least not physically.

Roofies.

But how? Her memories were returning, and the last thing Nicole recalled was hiking in Central Park. She hadn't stopped at a vendor for food or drink, and ate only what she packed herself.

The bridges and tunnels jammed, clotted, then were informally closed after the aliens appeared in May. You hiked to stay sane, as long as you could avoid the looters. Nicole didn't take any chances. She hadn't had to shoot anyone yet, but that didn't mean she wasn't ready.

She felt for her backpack.

Gone, of course.

Had she been abducted? No, the aliens took people using their smaller ships and beams of light. She'd seen nothing like that.

Maybe someone had come up from behind, put a chloroform rag across her mouth and nose. Someone must have been interested in a woman traveling alone.

Except Nicole had been looking around. Central Park had been divided by factions, and only one part — the part she'd traversed — had yet to be claimed by some gang or other. She was careful, same as always.

She didn't remember anyone. Had heard no footsteps, no rustling in the bushes.

Nicole remembered only the sphere.

About the size of a baseball, heavy as hell, cross-hatched with a grid of four parallel lines running across three different axes. The last thing she remembered was thinking it'd make a great bludgeon, much better than brass knuckles. And if she could throw it hard enough? Well. Something that *fuck-you* might be able to hurt the black dragons — the aliens with all of those teeth.

She remembered picking up the metal sphere. Hefting it. Then no more.

Was that *when they came at me with chloroform? When my attention fell on that weird thing in the grass?*

But no. One, Nicole would remember a struggle. Two, she'd have a headache upon waking. Taste or smell something funny. There had been the sphere, then inexplicably this.

An insect landed on her ear, but before she could raise her arm to swat it, something long and fuzzy entered her field of vision. A snake, but with too much girth, covered in hair. She recoiled, then she realized.

It's a ferret. That was the chatter of its claws on the metal floor.

As if that made sense. As if the presence of a rodent suddenly explained everything.

"He's scrawny, but friendly," said a voice.

Nicole bolted upright. Nearly pulled a muscle spinning to search for the voice, recognizing only now that she was downright terrified.

Breath surged in her throat. Heart pounded death in her ears. Everything was vibrant, too real, and entirely artificial. The ferret rushed away, frightened by her movement. The animal was half-starved, skin and bones, visibile ribs ringing its long body.

Nicole centered on a woman, not five feet away, sitting on a suspended bunk with her legs crossed beneath her. She had black hair, eyeshadow, and nail polish. Her eyes were bright green, bleeding like lights in the darkness. She wore a smart-cut suit that somehow straddled the look of outsider and professional. A punk who sold out. A reject working to buck the system from inside.

She looked ragged. Beat to hell. But Nicole sensed this was the woman's normal look, sedated on purpose. Far different than her own lethargy and exhaustion.

"Sorry. Thought you saw me." She yawned. "You sure did sleep a lot longer than I did."

The contrition sounded insincere. As if Nicole was a bother, her reaction impolite or out-of-line, and her demeanor cause for an apology.

"Who the hell are you?" Nicole asked, finally standing.

The room was small. All chrome and silver, hard edges insufficiently covered by scant furnishings, few wall adornments, lots of shelving, and plenty of crap — the ferret's open cage, a Cinco de Mayo skull with something written across its forehead, a calendar, a child's toy, a first-aid kit, even some of those little books you can use to choose a room's color. A small door across from the bunk clashed with the silver decor. Still metal, but fire-engine red. Closed, with some sort of lock above the knob. There was a clock on the wall, but the time felt wrong. The lone light fixture looked like the kind put in a building to artificially age it. The space didn't look lived-in and surely wasn't this woman's home.

"I'm Elyse. Who the hell are *you?*"

Nicole didn't answer. She continued looking around. The place looked like an efficiency apartment built by robots. Its creator had attempted to fill it with things humans tended to collect, but nothing was quite right. The knick-knacks were the kind that might be placed by a family, but their arrangement smacked of artifice. The woman's bunk looked comfortable enough, topped with a plush cushion and a throw, but it hung from the wall by a chain at the corners like in a prisoner's cell. And there were two sets of double-decker beds, both empty. They had a touch of canned personality — sheets and bedspreads in pink and blue, and a *My Little Pony* pillowcase.

How long had it been since that was even a thing?

Doors yawned open to the left and right. Two darkened rooms with more unseen inside. There were no windows. No natural light, no natural smells. They could be in the center of a building or on the ocean floor.

"Where did you find yours?" Elyse asked, shattering the stillness.

Nicole kept herself from jumping. She'd been so preoccupied with her study of the room, she'd forgotten the dour woman was there.

"My what?"

"Well, how did you get here? I've been trying to figure you out based on your clothes, but I've kinda got nothing."

"Have you just been staring at me while I lay on the floor?"

"Well, for as long as you were there." Elyse looked around. Nobody else was in the room. "The red door is locked." Her eyes went to the dark open doors. "I figured I'd wait and see if you wanted to go with for the rest. Didn't want to be rude, y'know."

Nicole said nothing. She hated people like this, and Elyse more than usual, with her stress hormones up. *Speak straight! Say what you mean!* That's where she and Mike always had their fights.

"I'm not going to bite, you know," Elyse said when Nicole didn't answer.

"Just let me think." Nicole rubbed her temples.

"Ah. Yes. *Think.* You do that." The woman leaned back and picked up a magazine. It had to be from the mid-2000s, judging by the cover and format. The only place with older periodicals might be a doctor's waiting room.

"Where are we?"

Elyse shrugged.

"What, so now you don't want to talk?"

"I don't know. How about we discuss our feelings?"

"Are you being a wiseass?"

"I'm not sure," Elyse said. "Is it funny?"

"I asked you where we are. What the fuck is this supposed to be, and who the hell do you think you are to—"

Elyse set the magazine in her lap suddenly enough to stop Nicole's talking. She stared. "Are you a three?"

"Excuse me?"

"You pretty much *have* to be a three or an eight."

"My husband says I'm a ten."

"Three, then." Elyse nodded, then returned to her magazine. No explanation.

Nicole waited a beat, then looked around. She eyed the red door first, drawn by its color. It was locked, but she didn't let Elyse see her because she didn't feel like a nonverbal *I-told-you-so*.

She shuffled into the right-side adjoining room. She could deal with Elyse later. Would have dealt with her now if she thought the annoying woman held any keys, but Nicole was good at reading people and knew she didn't. The sarcasm, the covert threat of withheld information ... yeah, Elyse was pointless.

The Elyses of the world were good for brainstorming and creative ideas, but too much of a pain in the ass for anything else. Talk to her much longer, and she'd try to rope Nicole into writing poetry. The insufferable, *life-sucks* kind where everyone lost everything and existence was futile.

The space was dark, so she crossed to the one opposite it. Also dark, but this time, Nicole flicked on the lights.

The room was exactly the same as the one she woke in, minus Elyse. She blinked, waiting for the oddity to register. Then she went the rest of the way in, scoping, pacing low.

The rapid whisk of a small brush seemed to follow her.

When Nicole looked down, she saw the ferret. They really were strange creatures. Weren't there some in her building at work? The fact that she didn't know meant it was time to tighten the reins once she got out of here. The aliens had left First Line alone, intruding little, treating Nicole's company with the *laissez faire* of a good government. Maybe the world wasn't going to Hell after all, despite what all the rebels and radicals seemed to say.

The ferret looked up at her. Rodent whiskers, rodent eyes. Didn't they have stink glands, like skunks? She'd better not kick it away — not unless she wanted a snoot full of ass.

The room even had identical knick-knacks. The skull, the toys, the book of paint chips. Same horrid decorator.

Same bright red door, with the same lock above it.

Nicole approached.

Then the lock keyed as if on its own, and the whole thing began to pound and rattle.

2

MARCUS'S HAND shot to his heart so fast, it looked like he was trying to catch a bullet.

Even deep breathing failed to settle him. When he woke in the strange metal room, he'd suffered five minutes of pure panic followed by the optimist's voice.

What a gift. A chance to meditate your way through it. To test yourself and chase calm.

Problem was, waking in a strange place without memory was more of an *Oh, shit!* situation than a personal test. Gilding the turd fooled no one.

"Ohmygod ohmygod," said the woman rushing toward him. She was in her lower fifties but with a teenager's energy. "Someone else! *Anyone* else. Holy shit, you have no idea how glad I am to see you. I've been running in circles I think, and some of these doors I swear are exactly the same. I eventually started marking them, but I'm sure my marks are moving, and I know how that sounds BUT!" She raised a finger in the air. "Patience paid off. Have you been through the blues yet?"

Marcus, only now prying his hand away from his heart, wondered if the woman was referring to his mood. *The blues.* What did that have to do with anything?

"Blues, greens, that taupe-like color," she chattered on, as if they were old friends returning to conversation *in media res.* "And did you see the fuchsia? Or was it magenta?"

"Who are you?" Marcus asked.

She shook his hand even though he hadn't offered it. "Deborah. Not Deb. Don't fucking call me Deb. My assistant is the only person who can call me Deb. All the shit he does for me, he has immunity. The kid could kill old people in front of me if he wanted, and I'd be cool with it."

Marcus wasn't sure what point elderly murder was meant to prove.

"And you are?"

"Marcus." Flabbergasted. So many questions, but he wasn't about to ask this nut job.

"Tim?"

"No, Marcus." Pause. "But please don't kill old people."

The woman laughed, apparently not frightened. Marcus, on the other hand, was scared enough to shit mangoes. He'd been about to step into the shower when he'd noticed a toy one his kids had dropped under the sink — a big metal ball of some sort. He'd gone to grab it, then the next thing he knew, he'd woken up here. At least whoever knocked him out and dragged him to this labyrinth had been thoughtful enough to dress him. It'd be so much worse making his way through this nightmare in the nude.

"Do you ..." Marcus stopped. People didn't really ask that kind of question. Not in real life. But he went on anyway, starting over. "Do you ... know where we are?"

"Red," she answered.

"Excuse me?"

He'd seen her only by the light of a few LEDs embedded in the ceiling above, but now she backed quickly off then hit something on the wall. Lights came on. She pointed at the room's far end.

"Red," Deborah repeated, pointing.

"I don't get it."

"I woke in blue," she explained.

"I still don't get it."

She sighed, then got behind Marcus and pushed. It was strange, being led. He was ordinarily in charge, usually the leader. The situation had stunned him, but this woman wasn't dulled at all.

Deborah pushed him into an adjoining room. He hadn't moved much. Marcus had started getting his bearings before she barged in and surprised the life out of him. But now, with the lights on, he could see there was an open door leading into a room just like the one he'd woken in, down to the sugar skull with *319* written across its skinless forehead on identical high shelves.

The light was on, Deborah having already been here. She squared his shoulders to another painted door, like in the last room, and said, "Red."

"Okay."

She wheeled him into the next room — the one Deborah must have come through one step before — then pointed at the same spot, at another closed door in the same place as the red one. Only now a different color.

"Yellow. I woke in blue." She jerked her thumb over her shoulder toward the room he'd just vacated. "Did you wake up there, in red?"

Curious now, Marcus walked back to the doorway

between rooms. He'd seen it, but wanted to see it again. And yes, one room had a yellow closed door at the end and the next — the one abutting the room he'd woken in — was red.

"The rooms aren't all the same. I thought they were at first, because they've got a lot of the same crap inside." She pointed to a stack of paper and business cards, some of which had been soiled by what looked like spilled ink, then to a framed photo showing a lot of poor-looking people behind a fence. "But actually, they're *slightly* different. Some have three adjoining rooms, even though most only have two. There's a fuckload. It's taken me a while to stop feeling like I'm going in circles. Or maybe I still am? I guess not, because I haven't run into you before, and I've been walking for *hours.*"

Something went bright in his mind. A different part than the frightful reptillian portion that had been steering his awareness so far, trapped and desperate for a way out. This new part was curious. Despite the oddity and the fact that he hadn't asked to be here — nor even knew where *here* was — Marcus was intrigued.

"What is this place?"

But the woman didn't seem to hear him. She paced the room, more distracted than stir crazy. Like a small child — only tall, blonde, and frenetic.

"How did you get here?" Marcus tried again.

"I've been thinking about that." She returned to his original room, then walked through it into the next. Marcus, who'd just been finding his senses, saw that room as a black hole in the wall. Now that Deborah was through and had flipped on the light, he could see it was another room like this one. Down to the same framed photo and the administrative mess on the corner desk. "Was the light on when you woke up?"

"Yes."

"Mine wasn't. I keep hearing things. Voices. I think there are other people in here. The echoes are weird — must be all the metal. But I've only heard people in the last ten minutes or so. Some yelling, some freaking right the fuck out. Like at the top of their lungs. You know that sound people make when—"

Marcus cut her off. Jesus. Her energy never slowed and her eyes refused to stay in one place. He knew someone like her, a man. The guy was brilliant but often walked around having forgotten to don socks or comb his hair. Half the time he had food on his face. All those brains, but zero direction. Wrangling him was like herding cats. Deborah seemed the same.

"What does that have to do with the lights being on or off?"

"Oh. Right." Into the next room, lights on, into the next, lights on, then back three rooms while Marcus tried to keep up. "Well, I turned my light off once I went into the next. Habit, from being at home, I guess. I found a marker and wrote my initials on the floor, but then I was back in that room later and the lights were on."

"Are you saying someone came through the room after you left but before you came back?"

"No. I made *this* route." She drew in the air, but to Marcus it was a vague set of gestures — some invisible diagram that made sense only to her brain. "The doors were on these walls, side-side, like a daisy chain. I measured with my feet and found that *that* end—" Pointing. "—is actually about an inch or two shorter than *that* end." Pointing at the opposite wall. "Do you see what I mean?"

"No."

"Well, obviously nobody could have come through

without me seeing them," she said, as if it was stupidly obvious. To Marcus, it wasn't. "I work a lot with CAD, or at least,
with people who use it."

"CAD?" He was thinking of what you called a man who
pinched asses and said inappropriate shit.

"Computer Aided Design."

"Are you an architect or something?"

"My company makes biohazard masks, respirators, and
filters."

"Like for painting?"

"N-95."

Marcus wasn't sure what that was, but didn't feel like
asking. He didn't like that Deborah made him feel dumb,
with her fast-talking and numbers and the way she thought
she'd mapped the entire place already. He'd graduated first
in his class, risen through the FDA ranks without palm-
greasing or kissing ass, and had an IQ of 164, which he'd
remembered from childhood because it kept coming up
when he worked with people who needed to know who they
were dealing with. Drone bureaucrats and wily ones still on
their way up. Marcus was the latter — an entrepreneur of
one, working as a free agent within the government.

Was there a word for that? If not, there should be.
Intrapreneur, perhaps.

Whatever N-95 was, Deborah's familiarity with
computer design, and the way it apparently made her confi-
dent in her spatial analysis of wherever they were, including
the supposed impossibility of someone sneaking by her.

"I still don't see what that has to do with the lights," he
told her.

"I left the room and they were off. I came back and they
were on. While I was exploring, turning lights on and off as
I went, I heard a *CHUNK!* sound, like something mechanical

slotting into place. Not heavy enough to be a big door opening. It sounded like someone hitting a bank of industrial lights, in a warehouse or something. My guess is that we were all supposed to wake up with the lights on, like you did. I just ... well, my brain doesn't let me sleep."

What, her brain was faster and better than his?

Marcus was methodical. *Needing* focus. *Needing* sleep. So details didn't get missed.

He'd heard something in what she said, but again felt resistant to ask.

We were all *supposed to wake with the lights on.*

All.

Rather than asking, Marcus filed that bit of information away. It was only the two of them, so far as he knew. She'd yet to mention anyone else. So ... was she in on something? Did she know more about this than she should?

"Last thing I remember was the ball."

Marcus, striding toward the next door, stopped. "What ball?"

"I found a silver ball in my yard, like a metal baseball. Looked like a *boule*. You ever play *boules*? It's like bocce, but French. I touched it, then ..." She shrugged.

Marcus said nothing. He didn't know *boules*, but he did know bocce. And the ball she'd described sounded an awful lot like the odd thing on the floor of his shower.

"What?" Deborah said. "What is it?"

"Nothing."

She turned, headed toward the unexplored room beyond.

"Where are you going?" Marcus asked.

"Through the maze."

"What makes you think we're not supposed to stay where we are?"

"Well, look around, Marcus. The room is slightly wedge-shaped, arranged in arcs or circles. Some of the rooms are shorter on one end and some are shorter on the other. But they must lead somewhere."

Marcus shook his head. "You don't know that they go anywhere."

"So you'd rather just sit still? Just wait to see what someone probes you with?"

Marcus sat up. Because yeah, this pretty much *had* to be an alien thing. If this was perpetrated by the aliens, did this woman really think *moving around* could change their fate?

And besides, Marcus didn't feel like going with Deborah's flow. He preferred a chance to call some of the shots ... looking at least a few seconds before leaping, of course.

"If it's really a maze," Marcus said, "and if you've really been walking for hours, there clearly isn't an easy way out. Moving will make us lost."

Deborah sighed.

"*What,* dammit?"

Deborah waited to see if the answer would become obvious. Then she said, "What's missing here?"

Marcus looked around. "A TV?"

"Plumbing. Water." Hands on her hips. "Think about it for a second. This has to be an Astral thing, right? So the way I see it, if the aliens wanted us dead, we'd already be dead. If they wanted us contained, they'd have closed the doors. Or they'd have put us ... well, *anywhere* that's not so lavishly and peculiarly decorated. But they put us *here.* There must be a reason. Who knows what that is. But either way, it involves us staying alive. Ergo, we have to move. And find water."

"Maybe it's torture. Maybe we're here to slowly die of thirst." Marcus stood and started walking.

"That's the wrong way."

"You don't know that. There's no 'right' or 'wrong' in here."

Faint illumination cut the darkness in Deborah's direction. A light coming on, far in the distance.

3

TYLER SAT IN SILENCE, watching the others. Evaluating them.

The woman, Miriam, was someone in authority, yet not comfortable with power. She wore the mantle of a person to whom others deferred, yet by nature seemed more servile than commanding.

The man, Kenneth, was looking for someone to blame. Not as a result of being angry — though he was. Not due to fear — he hid it well. And not even because he disliked disorder and needed answers —which also seemed to be true. It was more that he found the situation repugnant on a global level. The whole thing, to Kenneth, was *wrong*. Unfair. Nobody should be able to treat free citizens this way.

These were the things Tyler knew.

"Don't—" Kenneth said.

But Miriam ignored him and flipped a switch in the darkened room next to theirs.

The light came on. Kenneth, his order disobeyed, waited to see what foul thing might befall them after Miriam's reckless flipping. Nothing did.

Tyler observed, assessing Kenneth and Miriam. Studying his roommates of circumstance.

"I'm just turning on the light." Her arm was still in the next room, now illuminated, while the rest of her body remained within sight. She retracted the arm. "Thought we'd want to see where we are."

"We can already see where we are," Kenneth said.

"Where we're going, then."

"You don't know that's where we're going. *I* don't know that's where we're going, so how the hell can you?" He paced, thinking. "Maybe we should stay put. Maybe you should just *think* instead of deciding for everyone."

"There's no need for the attitude. I'm only trying to help."

"There's no need to flip random switches. You don't know what might happen! What if flipping that switch had ... had filled the room with poison gas?"

Miriam was pretty. Hair the color of stained maple, brown eyes, light freckles on darker skin. She did a thing with her mouth when amused and frustrated at once. Tyler saw it twice in the minutes they'd all been awake, and he saw it again now. The expression made her both patronizing and forgivable. It said, *You're ridiculous, but I don't judge you for it.*

Tyler's attention turned to the newly-illuminated room. It looked a lot like the one they were in now. Medium-sized, open doors on both sides, probably with a locked exit on the long wall, like the current room. *Creepy.*

"How about you, chief?" Kenneth turned to Tyler. "You wanna weigh in on this?"

"On what?"

"Someone put us here for a reason. Don't you think we ought to stay put so we can see what that reason is?"

"Or, maybe," Miriam said, also addressing Tyler, "it's a *better* idea to move so we *don't* have to find out why someone brought us here."

"How is moving around useful?" Kenneth asked. "Don't you think making them chase us will make it worse?"

Miriam shrugged. "You know, I'm just not as interested in the wants and needs of *those-who-kidnapped-us-and-stuck-us-in-a-box* as you are. I'm not as trusting of our captors. I don't think making this convenient for them is the way to go. But what do I know? This is my first time being abducted. So please." She waved at Kenneth in a way that seemed to say, *The mic is yours.* "Tell us your master plan. Tell us how to be useful."

Kenneth gestured to one of the shelves, at an open box of crackers. "We have food here."

Miriam looked into the next room. "Food here, too. Same box of crackers. Same ..." The strangeness of something finally hit her, as Miriam peered into the new room. "Same *everything*."

"There are beds."

"Beds over here too, Kenny."

"Don't call me Kenny." Kenneth fussed. "We should be voting on what to do. Majority wins."

"No offense, Kenny, but I'd rather not."

"Well, who the hell made *you* mayor?"

Miriam got a strange look. She was about to say something when there was a small sound from somewhere nearby. A squeaking. Maybe a door in need of oil or a balloon slowly leaking air.

Miriam turned to Tyler, looking for a tiebreaker. Her gaze ticked toward Kenneth as she spoke.

"Guys. Come on. We have to at least see what's here. The

doors are open. Don't you think they'd have closed them if they wanted us to stay put?"

"We have no idea what they'd want," Kenneth said. "That's my point."

"Nor who *they* are," Tyler added.

Though it had to be the aliens. Abductions abounded. Maybe this was where people went when they vanished.

"There's no water in here," Miriam said. "I don't know about you, but I'm already thirsty. Any guess what I was doing before I got here?"

Tyler looked her over. She was wearing something clingy, spandex or Lycra or whatever jogging tights were made of. Tyler and Kenneth weren't formal, but compared to Miriam, they looked ready for a soiree. Miriam's dark brown hair was in a pony tail and her running shoes were caked with mud.

"I was two hills from finishing my usual five-mile run. I don't carry water with me, and I was sweating a lot. I need to find something wet, sooner rather than later."

"You were running on a trail?" Tyler said.

"Yeah."

"I thought you said you were walking on a path."

"I was running. On a wooded trail."

"That's not what you said."

"What does it matter what I *said?*"

Tyler shrugged, not wanting to play his cards by answering.

But of course he had a response.

It mattered what she said — what *anyone* said — because a person's accuracy and truth revealed everything. He was calibrating his opinion, not yet convinced that Miriam and Kenneth weren't in on ... well, whatever this was.

And so he noted: *Miriam is either sloppy with her words, or she's lying.*

"I was in bed when it happened," Kenneth said.

"This late?" It wasn't a question so much as a judgment. Tyler could hear it in Miriam's voice. *What kind of lazy ass sleeps in all day?*

"I was in Australia," Kenneth answered.

"You got teleported all the way from Australia?"

"You don't have an accent," said Tyler.

"I was there for business."

"What kind of business?"

"What are you, a reporter?"

"I'm a software programmer," Tyler told him. "What are *you?*"

"What kind of software programmer?"

"I do pandemic modeling for the CDC."

"Great job with Phineas," Kenneth said.

"You referring to the pH1N2 outbreak?" Tyler asked.

"Of course I am."

"Oh, so you do know things," Tyler said. "And you still didn't tell us what you do. Why you were in Australia?"

"I don't know, T ..."

He trailed off. He'd forgotten Tyler's name already. Something to keep in mind about Kenneth. *Sloppy. Deceptive. Defensive. And, judging by his righteous attitude, a crusader who couldn't be bothered with details.*

"Tyler."

"Well I don't know, *Tyler,*" Kenneth said. "Maybe you can explain to me why you're acting like I'm under investigation?"

"I'm just asking questions."

"Maybe you should tell us," Miriam said.

"I was in Australia for a conference."

"International travel. In *this* day and age?"

"I'm a hospital administrator, okay? It's like The Red Cross. Alien ships don't bother our planes if our business is health and welfare. What's *your* story?"

He's deflecting.

"So you *don't* know."

"Know what?" Kenneth asked.

"You called me *mayor*," Miriam said.

"When?"

"Just now. You asked who made me mayor."

"Wait. Are you really a mayor?"

Miriam nodded. "Holiday Bend, Wisconsin. I thought you might have seen me on the news."

"Holiday Bend?" Tyler repeated.

"Don't tell me you've heard of it."

But of course he had.

Kenneth perked up as well. "My hospital is in Wilkings."

"What's Wilkings?" Tyler asked.

"It's about ten miles from Holiday Bend." Miriam eyed Kenneth before turning to Tyler. "Are *you* in Wisconsin?"

"No. I'm in Atlanta." But Tyler was interested. His roommates lived ten minutes from each other, yet one was brought in all the way from Australia? What kind of coincidence was that?

"Did we all ..." Kenneth scrunched his face. "Did we all come after touching a round metal—"

A sound came from the next room. Miriam, closest, peeked in. The sound repeated. A high-pitched squeak, like a chair's legs scraping against a polished floor.

"Guys," she said.

They gathered at the doorway.

The red door, formerly closed and presumably locked at the room's end, was open. Behind it was a small room, different from the other two they'd seen. No adornments or tchotchkes. Not a stick of furniture, so far as they could see.

But there was a small cage on the floor, filled with albino mice.

"Careful," Miriam said as Kenneth picked up the cage. The mice chattered, squeaking louder.

"Lab mice," Kenneth reported.

Tyler came closer. "Those aren't the kind of mice used in labs."

Miriam, shoehorned in, trying to see. Kenneth held the cage aloft, the mice protesting inside. There were nine of them. Red eyes. White fur. Pink noses.

"Those are feeder mice," Tyler went on. "The kind you give to snakes."

Kenneth shook his head and opened his mouth to speak.

But the door closed behind them before he could, dropping from a pocket in the wall like a guillotine. Kenneth went to it, tried the lock, found nothing. Miriam went to the other door across from it. Black, and also unyielding.

Tyler swallowed. Small spaces weren't his thing.

A ten-by-ten bare room, no windows, two closed doors.

Like a cell.

Miriam tried one. Kenneth set down the cage, then tried the other.

They were locked in.

4

"WHAT THE HELL?"

Shouting.

Ian startled some, Zach a little less. It took him a moment to make out Ian's words. His focus was on the sugar skull — the kind of thing you bought downtown during *Dia de los Muertos*. He'd seen skulls like this before. Bejeweled, brightly colored, cheerful more than morose. But this one had the number 319, and that number rang a resonant bell.

Ian sprinted halfway across the large room, then stalled, as though trying to figure out where the shouting had come from. The yelling and pounding had already stopped. "Did you hear that?"

"I ... yeah." Zach set the sugar skull down, eyeing it. The room was almost circular, shelves and desks scattered hither and yon between the doors, breaking only at the tiny kitchen with its sink, empty refrigerator, inoperable stove-top, and incongruous toilet in case either of them wanted to shit beside the Frigidaire.

The few non-metal things stuck out like bashed thumbs — like that freaky skull. They'd already looked through all the paperwork, business cards, and first aid kit with a big red cross on the front. They joked about snuggling with the teddy bear, then tried to solve the equation on a whiteboard behind one of the beds. They'd sorted through the pile of what looked like bulk cargo, but the wooden boxes were empty and the burlap bags had more bags inside. The ropes, in that same corner, were only ropes — nothing heavy or useful on them, like block and tackles.

Ian couldn't stop staring at a blown-up photo — a bunch of Mexicans behind a chain-link fence, guards with guns visible in the distance.

"Where did it come from?" Ian asked. "The pounding and shouting? One of the doors?"

It came again before Zach could answer.

Ian zeroed in, stood with his ear to the door that seemed to be talking. The black one, next to the white one. To the black door, he said, "Hello?"

The shouting increased, but without his ear to the door, Ian couldn't make out any words. He waved to Zach. "I hear people on the other side. Come help me."

"With what? I work for the government. I don't know how to pick locks."

"Just …" Ian waved again with frustration.

The doors had no hinges. A crowbar could maybe wedge one open, but they didn't have one. And so far, they'd tried every one of the twenty-five doors ringing the room, including the previously-silent one Ian was pressed against now. They were trapped, and there wasn't any reason to believe they could leave this room without someone letting them go.

"Where did we hear someone before?" Zach asked.

"Who cares? They're over here now."

"The first room sounded like women. *That* sounds like men. Or at least *a* man."

"I don't know what to tell you, but can you get the hell over here?"

Zach didn't remember coming here. He had reached into his home recycle bin for the strange object nestled in its center, then woke up on a bunk next to an unconscious stranger twenty feet away. They'd tried all they could to break out in the hour or so since. How was he supposed to help Ian now?

"Which door was it? Where we heard the woman. I at least want to mark it." Zach looked back.

"The red one," Ian said, still with his ear to the door.

"Which red one? There are three."

"The right-side one. I think."

"You think? Or you know?"

"I know. Now will you *get over here?*"

Not at all convinced, Zach trotted to the nearest shelf, grabbed the small brown teddy bear, then tossed it sidearm toward the right-side red door.

"Hello?" Zach said when he reached Ian, projecting through the door.

"Hello?" Ian echoed.

The door shook with the pounding of what Zach presumed were fists. He could hear the shouters a bit better, but not enough to make out words. There were *three* voices. Two men and a woman.

"Get your fingers in there, Zach."

"There's no room for fingers."

"Just do it!"

Zach did, but nothing happened.

"Dammit, Zach!"

"I'm doing all I can."

"Pull!"

"Calm down, will you?"

Instead of calming, Ian backed up then kicked the door.

"That's not going to help," Zach said as Ian winced, his toe mashed.

"I'm just trying to get us out of here."

"I am too. But getting upset won't help at all."

"I'm not upset."

"You're anxious. You're freaking out."

Ian kicked the door again. *"I'm not freaking out!"* He closed his mouth, lowered his protesting hands, then said, "Fine."

"We have to concentrate," Zach told him.

"I can do that. I'm good at focusing and making plans." Ian had short hair, basically a non-military brush cut, and bright blue eyes. His trying to grandstand had, in its way, been funny. Ian struck Zach as a good-guy — a buddy who stuck by you and ultimately did what he was told.

"Then let's think," Zach said.

Which was hard, with the people behind the black door shouting louder, kicking and slapping on their side. One phrase finally clear: *We're trapped!*

But Zach and Ian had been trapped for a while. These folks made it sound like a recent development.

They weren't trapped, but now they are.

But how? And why did it matter?

His gaze went to the sugar skull on its perch. To the painted numbers on its forehead.

319.

He was good at consensus. Good at getting people to listen. Good at getting diverse people to agree, to make their peace, to see common ground. Like that time when—

319.

Oh. *That's* where he knew that number from. Not a reminder he wanted, even if it was only a coincidence.

Guilt came.

Then rationalization.

"Ian. What if instead of trying to break the door open, we—?"

Zach didn't get to finish the thought because the black door slid sideways. Three people tumbled into the room, red-faced and screaming.

5

WITH HER EAR pressed against the red door, Elyse could hear the sound change in the room beyond.

The door was either thick or otherwise impervious. All they'd gotten before now were low mumbles that probably weren't even words. Elyse blamed Nicole for the lack of clarity. When the door rattled that first time, Nicole dragged them both away. From bossy to coward in seconds.

During that wasted time trying to open doorways that only led to more similar if not identical rooms, the whoever-it-was on the other side was probably yelling, proving themselves as prisoners rather than captors. Why would their captors rattle a door instead of simply opening it?

"I'm telling you," Elyse said. "There's people over there."

"So what?"

"Well ..." It was too baffling a response to wrap her mind around. Nicole's wanting to run from their only lead in this labyrinth made zero sense to Elyse. And she thought of herself as an individualist? Nicole made Elyse look like the entertainment director on a cruise ship.

"Well?" Nicole echoed.

"Well, they might be able to help us." Elyse banged on the door, sensing a number change on the other side. Since returning to the room where they'd heard the door rattle and shake, they'd been in recon mode. Listening only. Now, hearing a commotion on the other side, Elyse wanted to engage. There were one or two voices before, but now she heard many.

"Hey!" she yelled.

"Keep your voice down," Nicole said.

Elyse glanced back to overtly ignore her and caught Nicole brushing lint from her sleeves, picking at the creases. Her activewear beat Elyse's to death. Nicole was apparently hiking in three hundred bucks' worth of Yoga Bear. Elyse tossed on threadbare Umbros and a ratty tee when she was forced to exercise. And Nicole was also wearing makeup. Like a bitch.

"At least put that thing down," Nicole said when Elyse banged and shouted again.

"I'm distraught. I need human contact." Elyse cradled the emaciated ferret in the crook of her non-pounding hand.

"It's not a human."

"You're sure *you* are?"

"Very funny. I'll bet it's hard to be so hilarious while also acting like you're depressed."

"I'm just depressed about society. Depressed about White Privilege." Elyse banged on the door again. She looked back. "Don't you care if we get out of here?"

Nicole rolled her eyes. "Please. I have people. Whoever did this is *fucked.*"

"I see. So your lawyer is going to save you." She rammed her fist against the metal. "HELLO? WE CAN'T OPEN THE DOOR!"

Nicole said something else, but Elyse didn't hear it. Her attention was on the voices, which were ... *yes* ... coming closer.

"You don't even know who's over there," Nicole said.

But now Elyse just wanted to punch her. Or quietly *subvert* her, that was more Elyse's style. Nicole had her pegged as some sort of burnout goth, probably because she'd done the black-paint thing and had always looked ten years younger than she was. It would be delicious to reveal her identity, but that was best saved for later. Especially since, during their thirty or so minutes together, Nicole had taken every opportunity to bring up her irrelevant successes. She was EVP somewhere. Her husband was eight years younger than her and had six-pack abs. She had built one company before selling it and helped take another public. All sensible conversation when trapped in some weird kind of prison, right? And yet about Elyse, Nicole knew nothing. Seemed to recognize her face, but hadn't yet placed it. Meanwhile, Elyse had been weighing an EVP's salary, trying to decide if it could be anywhere near her own. Probably not. Elyse was in the public eye, with a contract and guaranteed air time — a clause that upped her earnings in line with the ratings.

Nicole stood with crossed arms, trying to affect being in charge.

"You know," Elyse said, "you don't have to stay with me. If you think your plans are so great, feel free to—"

She was leaning against the red door. It slid sideways, and she staggered through. A man with a mustache tried to catch her, but she hit the ground anyway.

A man wearing a gray hoodie and a buzz cut leaned down at the same time as a dark-skinned woman. They regarded each other, half-smiled at the near collision, then the man backed off to let the woman help Elyse to her feet.

"Are you okay?"

Elyse considered saying she'd slammed her elbow hard, but she was still holding the ferret and Nicole would hear her response, so she said, "I'm fine. But thank you."

"What is that thing?" asked a man in what looked like pajamas. Despite his nighttime attire, he still managed to look ready for a board meeting.

"Oh! It's a ferret," Elyse answered. "I call him Morpheus."

"Why do you have a ferret?" asked a man in business casual.

"We woke up back there." She pointed. "And there was a ferret. That's all I know."

"I'm Miriam," said the woman.

"Elyse."

She turned to Nicole. "Miriam."

"Nicole."

"Nice to meet you, Nicole."

And Nicole said, "Hmm."

Five people. Four men and one woman.

Miriam they'd met.

Ian in the hoodie.

Kenneth in pajamas.

Zach in business casual.

And Tyler, officious in his bushy mustache.

"Seven of us," Tyler said.

"Do you have door controls on this side?"

"Actually, we" — Ian indicated himself and Zach — "thought we were locked in. Then that black door opened, and these three came in."

"We were locked in, too. In a room not like any of the ..."

Kenneth trailed off, looking around. Elyse was doing the same thing. And so was Nicole.

This wasn't like all the other rooms. It had a kitchen, plus a load of crap in the corner. They had the world's most immodest toilet, plenty of room, and doors of every color. She and Nicole had seen dozens of identical rooms while exploring, but this one looked like the hub.

Or *a* hub — given its size, there could be many within the maze.

"Water," Miriam said, following Elyse's and Kenneth's gazes. She went to the micro kitchen, then turned on the faucet. When water came out, she sighed with relief then panned it into her mouth.

The others told their stories. Zach and Ian had woken in the big round room, trapped. Until a door opened across the room. That's when Miriam, Kenneth, and Tyler all joined them. The three newcomers were wandering through identical rooms that sounded like what Elyse and Nicole had seen, then managed to open one of the colored doors and ended up trapped in yet a third type of room, maybe ten by ten.

"We went in because of the mice," Tyler said.

"Mice?"

On cue, Morpheus leaped from Elyse's arms. She tried to catch the ferret but caught only a glancing blow.

He ran directly at a small cage near the other open door, which for some reason was full of white mice.

"There were mice just sitting around?" Elyse asked.

"On the floor," Miriam said. " Just ... there."

"Why?"

"Who knows?"

Morpheus click-clacked toward the mice on clawed feet. He nosed the cage, found resistance, then laid on his haunches to watch them. Or at least, Elyse *thought* the ferret was a he.

"So ... does anyone remember how they got here?" asked the boring-looking man. Zach.

Their stories had only one common denominator, but it was a big one. Everyone remembered reaching for a metal ball with lines cut into its surface. Except for Kenneth, but the group theorized that if he was sleeping, it could have been in his bed, and he could have rolled onto it.

Other than that, anecdotes were all over the place, with nothing apparent in common.

Kenneth, a hospital administrator, and Miriam, a small-town mayor, were from Wisconsin. Tyler lived in Atlanta and worked for the government. Zach worked for the government as well, but his position sounded impressive to Elyse. *Secretary of Health and Human Services.* He mentioned the president once or twice, but not in a name-dropping way. Unlike Nicole, who needed everyone to know exactly how successful she was. Ian worked in New York, for Overlook Media. A scattered set for sure.

"What about you?" Miriam asked Elyse. Of the group, Miriam was easily the most engaging. Tyler focused inward, Kenneth projected the same hardness as Nicole, and the others were just sort of there. Except for Zach. He became the referee, directing conversational traffic, making sure each person got their turn.

"Oh. I'm ... I'm on TV."

She was about to elaborate, but Ian snapped then pointed right at her.

"That's where I know you from!"

"What?" Nicole swiveled to Elyse. "From where?"

"She's on *Wake Up!*" Ian finished.

Nicole's expression was precious.

"Jesus Christ, I thought you looked familiar. I watch you while I have my coffee most mornings. I couldn't place you, so out of context, but ..."

"You work for Overlook and you watch *us*?"

"Sure." Ian shrugged. "My boss likes to know our enemy. How else can we combat your liberal bullshit?"

He smiled so she'd know he was only joking, though really he wasn't. *Wake Up!* leaned left while pretty much every show on the Overlook network leaned right. Was that what this was about? Politics? Elyse knew — more from personal experience than the news — the Astrals were interested in human conflict. They set up those mind-reading stones, they'd dropped bombs into rioting cities to tell them to get along or die.

They were still standing by the door. After deciding all the rooms were the same, Elyse wanted to explore this very different venue. This room had a rainbow, rather than a lone colored door. Instead of beds and desks, this room had plumbing. Water to drink.

Elyse nodded to the others then strode toward the kitchen. She stepped on something squishy and almost tripped. Recovering, Elyse looked back to see what nearly tripped her — a small brown teddy bear wearing a little blue bowtie.

She felt the air leak from her lungs. Elyse had been wearing a newly optimistic half-smile, but the toy stole all the tension from her face. She picked it up, held it. Stared at it. The fur was matted, as if from a child's love. The material was soft, worn almost smooth. The nose was scuffed, and one ear was worn, as if from chewing.

"Why was this on the floor?"

The others looked up.

Elyse held the bear for all to see. "Whose is this? Who put it on the ground?"

Shrugs and uncertain expressions.

"Who!" Elyse barked.

"I ... I did," Zach said. "I wanted to mark the door so we didn't forget which one we heard you behind."

"Where did you get it?"

"Why?"

"Where did you get it?"

"On the shelf!" Zach pointed.

Kenneth peered over her shoulder, inspecting the bear with raised eyebrows. "Oh, yeah. There was one of those in our room, too."

"All the rooms we went through," Miriam added.

Elyse stared at Zach, then at the bear.

There was an elevator inside her, plummeting to the bottom floor. Then past it, into a chasm.

"Elyse?" Nicole's hand settled on her shoulder. Strange but welcome.

Anything but this.

"What's going on here?" Ian asked.

Tyler was watching her. Studying her.

She looked at the bear.

She knew this toy.

"This belonged to my nephew," Elyse said.

6

KENNETH WATCHED ELYSE, wondering at her angle.

What was her game? She had to be wrong, or possibly lying. The bear couldn't belong to anyone, if for no other reason than there was a bear just like it in each room. They were stock from a well-worn lot, same as that photo of immigrants, the identical stack of papers, and that weird Mexican skull with the number on it. The same miscellany repeated in every room, down the rabbit hole into infinity.

His gaze went to a shelf nearby, then to the book of paint chips. It was open to a certain section, some of the colors marked. A few had X's and others had checkmarks. One was looped with a circle.

There was a loud bang as newcomers entered the room.

Kenneth grabbed a hammer from the pile of ropes and cargo. Their captors would reveal themselves eventually, and he planned to be ready when they did.

But the newcomers weren't aliens. It was a severe-looking man in jeans and a woman whose presence was deafening.

"Here they are," she announced.

The woman was tall, blonde, and radiated energy. She didn't look frightened, surprised, or even put out. Her greeting sounded exasperated more than anything. *Shame on the seven of you, eluding us for so long.*

The man held back, sticking to the doorframe, wary. He was either suspicious or one of those people with resting mean face. Kenneth knew the type, one of his department heads at Region General had the same demeanor. The new man would be hard to impress, and it'd always seem like those around him were doing everything wrong.

The woman went to Nicole first.

"Hi. Deborah."

"Nicole," she said, seeming confused by the woman's casual familiarity.

Deborah approached Kenneth next. She seemed to be going in order. Miriam, Zach, and Ian were too mild to be in charge, and Elyse had the weird thing with the teddy bear. The man with the mustache — Tyler, was it? — had sequestered himself in the corner, silent, eyes attentive.

"Deborah."

"I'm Kenneth."

"We heard you from like twenty rooms away."

To Kenneth, this sounded like some sort of accusation or blame. Their party was too raucous. And shame on them, they hadn't remembered to invite Deborah and her bodyguard.

"Oh," was all Kenneth could think of to say.

"That's Marcus."

Marcus came forward. He also went to Nicole first, then Kenneth, before kind of nodding at the rest. He wasn't the silent type like Tyler. He was cautious — a hunter who methodically closed off his prey's exits before moving in for the kill. The room was assessed, and now he was emerging from his shell. His shoulders went back, a civil expression claimed his face. He stood a bit taller in front of Kenneth, as if in subconscious challenge.

More introductions. Kenneth watched carefully. Their mood bothered him. The woman's manner craved control, her bustling promised rash action without forethought. High-energy chaos. The man wasn't chaotic at all. He seemed the kind of person who'd wait for his moment, then take charge. The room's body language was already, after just sixty seconds, deferring to them.

Kenneth was beginning to figure all of this out. He had been paying attention to nuance. The repeating elements couldn't be coincidence, and there was a pattern to the rooms he hadn't yet solved. They needed to proceed slowly and with deliberate order, not fly off half-cocked.

He scanned the room while the same information repeated for Deborah and Marcus. Nothing new. Deborah had a theory about the rooms forming a spiral, but anyone with a brain had figured that out already. Their present room was some sort of a hub — one of several, perhaps. It wasn't coincidence they'd all ended up there. They'd been steered, in part by the labyrinth's geography itself.

Marcus broke his silence, and Deborah played off him. He barfed theories and she added flavor, waving her arms and pitching a dozen half-formed ideas about where they were and how to get out. They had it all figured out, it seemed.

From where Kenneth was standing, the only question was whether or not the other seven of them were planning to hop aboard before the Marcus/Deborah train left without them. Because rest assured, that particular engine had a full head of steam and was going *somewhere*.

Kenneth, studying, searched for his patterns.

The rooms.

The repeating elements, along with those that did not.

Like the cargo pile. The ropes. The water supply and toilet. And the single starving ferret.

Marcus and Deborah hadn't opened a new door into the large room. They'd entered through the same door as Kenneth's group, having followed lights since Miriam started flipping switches. Kenneth thought back, decided he'd heard their pursuers as they navigated the maze.

His gaze went to the strangely familiar paint chips.

And Ian, now drifting from the others, studied the framed photo of all those people behind a fence. The same one Kenneth noticed earlier and had seen Ian eyeing, as well.

Just as Zach's eyes were on the sugar skull, *319* written in jewels across its brow.

"There's a whiteboard back here," Deborah said, already distracted and meddling. She pulled it out. The thing was full of writing and equations — the *same* writing and equations that Kenneth's discerning eyes had seen on the other buried whiteboards. A copy of something written by hand.

"And *someone's* been teaching math," Deborah added, bringing it into the light.

Kenneth watched everything and saw it all.

The way Tyler's head ticked up then away, filing the whiteboard in his internal filing system, as he sat there judging everyone. The way he stared too long, his mouth a slightly open before looking away.

Nobody saw it happen. Nobody saw the way Tyler recognized something in all those scribbles, then pretended the whiteboard meant nothing.

Nobody except Kenneth.

He stood and came forward. Kenneth was about to

investigate — to pull at a few of the loose ends he was coming to believe his roommates were concealing — when Deborah's voice caught his attention.

She was like a toddler, full of energy with nowhere to go. The constant stream was abrasive, rubbing against Kenneth's insistence that this mess be handled carefully and right. He hoped their captors didn't give them a bomb to diffuse, because Deborah would leap on the thing without asking, cutting red and blue wires just to see what might happen.

Right now, she was squatting in front of Morpheus, petting him and saying, "You want one of these, don't you?"

Without hesitation, Deborah reached for the cage.

"Wait," Kenneth said.

"Ferrets eat mice." Her hands were already on the latch. "This poor guy is starving."

"Hang on a minute," Tyler told her.

But Deborah's hand was already inside the cage, grabbing one of the mice by its tail.

"Don't," Miriam said.

Deborah shook her head. "Don't be ridiculous. One ferret. One cage full of mice. It's obviously what they're here for."

Just as Kenneth was about to weigh in, Deborah's clumsy hand rattled the cage. The mouse squirmed in her fist. She held it fast, but then her left hand tipped the works forward. Two mice escaped before she could close the door.

"Shit."

"Goddammit, nice job." Nicole backed up then climbed onto one of the bunk seats.

Deborah stuffed the dangling mouse back into the cage. She darted after one mouse while Morpheus chased the other. It would have been amusing if their circumstances weren't so dire.

"Cut it off!" Marcus shouted, pointing to direct the others. "No, not that way!"

The ferret raced its quarry in furry circles until the mouse was finally cornered.

Morpheus leapt. The mouse squeaked. Kenneth watched the ravenous animal rip into its prey as the room worked to catch the second escapee.

Deborah scrabbled, ducking low, climbing under desks and bunks and chairs. There were no mouseholes in all the metal. The dumb white thing kept hitting impassable corners. Ian guarded the black door and Miriam guarded the red one, ensuring it didn't escape.

Why? Kenneth wondered.

Tyler moved only when Marcus pointed at him, directing traffic, telling him to go here or there. Elyse still clutched the bear. Nicole sat on her perch, barking orders. Zach did little, moving at a snail's pace as if he could catch any mice that way.

"Ken!" Marcus barked. "Seriously!"

"It's Kenneth."

"Kenneth! Seriously!" Marcus pointed at something happening too fast for Kenneth to respond, then rolled his eyes and groaned when he failed to intercept.

A furry white bullet shot past his feet then under the desk with all the papers.

Tyler's attention was still on the whiteboard, maybe solving equations to move his mind away from the mess.

Deborah, chasing the mouse, rammed her ass into the desk's chair.

Zach sidestepped, missed, collided.

Two bodies nearly hit the floor, but instead Deborah

skittered away and Zach's momentum slammed him into the chair, which banged against the desk and upset the fragile administrative ecosystem. Papers and cards rained to the ground in a wood-pulp waterfall around her.

"You know what?" Marcus said. "It's easier to just let it go."

Kenneth looked him. "How do we do that?"

"Get away from the doors."

"What if it's in here for a reason?" Tyler asked.

"It's a mouse. It's here for the ferret, if anything."

"Morpheus!" Deborah shouted, stabbing a finger into the air. She moved from mouse to ferret, following on all fours, then got the animal's long body in her hands.

"You want another, right?" she asked it.

"You know," Elyse said, "maybe instead of just—"

"Move," Nicole said, finally off her throne. She'd been watching Marcus and Deborah take charge, and clearly wanted some power for herself. She reached out a manicured hand and pushed Elyse aside.

Elyse shot her daggers, but Nicole was oblivious.

"Put it there," Nicole said, to Deborah, meaning Morpheus.

The ferret shot into the pile of cargo and ropes, immediately flushing out the little white mouse. One or the other upended something in the pile — ink, maybe? — and blue liquid streamed from some unknown place onto the floor. Also onto the mouse, turning the prey half blue, nearly missing the ferret. Its tiny feet chattered across the metal floor, leaving marks of indigo.

"It's making a mess," Kenneth said.

"Let me help you." Miriam offered her hand.

Nicole pushed her away. "I'm fine."

"There!"

Ian pointed. The blue mouse re-emerged, the ferret seeing it too late. The mouse ran for the door, feet finding purchase, the ferret scrabbling behind, its traction inferior.

"GET IT!"

And Kenneth, directed by a shouting Marcus, tried. But three feet from his quarry, a beam of green light lanced from somewhere unseen and struck the mouse. A second later, the furor was gone, and the room was stunned into silence.

"Guys." Tyler finally said. "Guys!"

Not just alert. Fear. Almost panic.

A panel had opened on the wall above the desk. There were symbols and ciphers behind it, rendered mechanically but changing with the precision of Swiss engineering.

Each swap of symbols came with a subtle but heavy mechanical noise. The sound of a stamping plate, or great masses coming together.

Chunk.

Chunk.

Chunk.

About one beat per second.

"It's a clock," said Tyler.

And it was, Kenneth felt certain. Even if the numbers were unfamiliar, they were looking at a clock — counting down to zero with some unknown time remaining.

More sounds. Not from the clock, but from the open rooms beyond the red and black doors.

Ian poked his head through the black one, then turned back to the group, his face pale.

"The maze," he said. "It's changing."

7

Tyler was aware that the opening and closing doors merited his attention, but he couldn't bring himself to pay it. Not with his eyes on the thing that had bugged him twice already.

He had thoughts about what was happening, even though he'd yet to postulate hows and whys. Collecting and analyzing facts then finding the truth was his specialty. The rooms held patterns ... along with the strange, deceptively insignificant items and changes.

And now, in a one-two-three combo, they'd seen a mouse annihilated — wasn't even hair left — something that was obviously a timer was now counting down, and the labyrinth of rooms had begun to shift. All very interesting, and all very troubling. But in the end, only data.

Just like the information on the whiteboards — repeated in at least two rooms so far.

$$dy/dt = k \cdot y \, (N - y)$$

. . .

WITH INITIAL CONDITION

$$y(0) = N/10$$

AND INTERMEDIATE CONDITION

$$y(1) = N/5.$$

SO FAMILIAR. So academic. But the rest of the board, of course, was the problem. There was basic theory ... and then there was what had *actually happened* during the incident two and a half years ago. The event surprised them all — and only Tyler knew that without one little mistake, the world could have been surprised a lot less.

The mistake was on the whiteboard, plain as day.

A fist gripped his chest. The air was too thin.

Someone knew.

Not far from Tyler, Marcus was on his knees in the pile of spilled paperwork, giving a small card his undivided attention. His eyes darted as he slipped it into his pocket — a covert move nobody was meant to see.

Marcus looked at Tyler.

Tyler looked at Marcus.

Information passed between them, but neither could have said what it was.

"What do you mean, *the maze is changing?*" Nicole asked.

Ian paced, uneasy, darting from door to door. His discomfort made him appear even younger than he was. He struck Tyler as a kid in a hoodie, upset by something he neither understood nor could control. But was that true? Did he have no control? Hadn't Ian said he worked for Overlook Media? And hadn't they done that series of scaremongering campaigns that complicated Tyler's predictions, even without the mistake?

"I *mean*," Ian snapped while passing Nicole on his way from red door to black. "*The maze ... is changing.*"

"Where do you think you're going?" she demanded.

Ian ignored her. Chatter, among the others, multiplied out of control.

"Hey," Marcus echoed, standing, calling for Ian. "*Hey!*"

Ian ignored him, too.

"*HEY!*" Top of his lungs, a room-stilling shout.

This time, Ian stopped.

Marcus said, "Everyone be quiet. I need to think."

Ian looked at Marcus. "Just you?"

"Fine. *All of us* can think." Marcus was the kind of guy to realize the world had other people.

"What's there to think about?" Elyse asked.

"What all of this means."

Nicole's hooded gaze bore into Marcus. "Who says it means anything?"

He nodded, presumably to himself, before speaking. But the others still waited, deferring to the room's new gravity. Outside, doors continued to slide and thump, some closer, others farther away. Inside, the big alien clock shifted glyphs, ticking with its steady *chunk-chunk-chunk.*

"Start with the mouse," Marcus finally said.

"What *about* the mouse?" Kenneth asked.

Everyone looked to Kenneth.

But Marcus spoke to the group. "What happened with the mouse tells us two things. First, it says that whoever put us here is *present*. They haven't just stuck us in a box and run off. Second, they're not entirely objective. They're *moderating* us — wanting a certain outcome rather than simply seeing what happens."

"Oh," Kenneth scoffed. "You figured *all of that* out, did you?"

Marcus turned to Kenneth. "The mouse got loose. When we couldn't catch it, someone 'caught' it for us."

"That could have been automated," Kenneth said.

"Why?" Marcus asked. "And *how*, if that laser thingy shot the mouse instead of us?"

"You don't know anything." Kenneth sneered and turned to anyone who'd meet his eye, though few did.

"What's *your* big idea, then?" Marcus asked.

"I don't have a big idea. But it's dangerous to presume anything about—"

"Then why don't you keep your fucking comments to yourself?"

Kenneth took a step. Marcus turned to face him.

Zach shoved himself between the men. "Let's all just calm down."

Quiet, between ticks of the clock and the sliding of doors. The air reeked of burned fur.

"He's right."

Everyone looked at Tyler. So far, he'd been in the background, quietly working the puzzle. He didn't like attention. Things were easier when you were a fly on the wall. But as all eyes encouraged him, he went on anyway. "They intervened once we stopped doing what we're supposed to be doing."

"Who's 'they'?" Nicole asked. "And what the hell makes you think we're 'supposed' to be doing anything?"

"I don't know who brought us here or what they want. But look at what happened. We were fine on our own. The mouse escaping was a chaotic element." He pointed at the knocked-down paperwork, the framed photo hanging askew, the bunks they'd run into while chasing. "Once there was chaos, whoever's running this ... this *thing* ... intervened."

"You can't know that," Miriam said.

"I know that chaos ruins an experiment. Unless it *is* the experiment."

Elyse laughed, the sound was too loud to be genuine.

"I know a thing or two about chaos," Tyler said, his voice flat.

"Okay. Let's say you're right, just for a second." Zach looked around. "What does it mean?"

"Our captors have opinions about what we're doing in here. Their intervention implies moral action."

"*Moral?*" Miriam repeated.

"Meaning there's a right and a wrong outcome. A difference between *going according to plan* and *gone off the rails*. If they were only *studying* us, they'd watch and see what we did. But *that?*" Tyler pointed to where the mouse had vanished. "We're being *tested,* not studied."

Kenneth scoffed.

"You don't believe me?" Tyler asked.

"*The mouse* was fried. *It* was judged, not us."

Tyler thought he'd have to explain again — at toddler level, this time — when Marcus spoke.

"I was thinking the same thing."

Oh? You were? Tyler resisted the urge to shoot Marcus a look, seeing as they were on the same side. But he also saw his words for what they were — an attempt to claim some credit for Tyler's discovery.

"*Who's* testing us?" Elyse looked even gothier than before, despite her clutching that little brown bear like a totem.

"The Astrals, obviously," Ian said.

"You don't know it's the Astrals." Nicole shook her head.

"*Of course* it's the Astrals. Who the hell else could do something like this? The government?" Elyse looked at Zach, who said he had the president's ear.

"Don't underestimate the government," Deborah said.

Tyler scoffed. "*Please.* Alien abductions used to be a joke. Until the Astrals came and made them a fact. They've been testing us since the first ships arrived. The takings, the weirdness of the people who come back, the stones they put up in lines everywhere to read people's minds—"

"Actually, the alien stones *open* people's minds," Zach said. "Get two people together while they're close enough to the stones, and they'll be able to hear *each other's* thoughts."

It was a non sequitur, irrelevant to his point. Tyler stopped, patronizing, and waited for the awkward moment to pass. In the quiet gap, Deborah gestured at Zach. "See? *Government.*"

"The stones," Tyler continued, "let them spy on our thoughts. The bombs they dropped, like in Ukraine and that one in Austin, go off only if those cities don't stop fighting."

"So they're morality police. Kindergarten cops."

"*It's not a tumor!*" said Miriam, but nobody laughed.

"In a way," Tyler answered. "I've researched the Astrals extensively. There's a growing theory that all of this — not us here, but the entire occupation — is about judgment. They've been here for months. So why haven't they formally invaded? Why haven't they taken us over, established their own puppet governments?" He tapped his knee. "It's because they want to see what we do on our own, so they can sit back and judge our actions. That's why they've let us reestablish so many of our routines. Why they practically encouraged us to forget they were there and get back to business. We're an ant farm to the Astrals."

"Bullshit." Kenneth shook his head. "They abducted tons of people, destroyed cities, let those fucking ... *things* ... loose in the countryside ..."

"At first. But then most of their activity backed off, and now they're only observing." Tyler gestured at the room. "They're testing us, I promise."

Zach said, "If this is a test, why no shocks or treats?"

"They can test by just watching what we do. There don't need to be punishments and rewards." Tyler shifted, pulling up his mental list of observations. "Except that there *have* been rewards. Like the doors."

"What *about* the doors?" Miriam asked.

"When we were trapped, a door opened."

"Because they opened it." Kenneth nodded to Zach and Ian.

"We didn't do anything," Ian said. "We've been trying to get out of this room since we got here. It only opened when you opened it."

"We didn't open it." Kenneth shook his head.

They looked at each other. Tyler could see Nicole and Elyse trading glances as well, probably wondering about their own open door.

"Almost everything in this place is repeated in every room," Tyler said. "One of the few exceptions is that ferret. Why only one?"

Marcus shrugged. "That doesn't mean anything. Why just one kitchen?"

"The kitchen is the only source of water. We needed it to stay alive."

"We didn't even know it was here."

"Zach and Ian did," Tyler said. "They started where there was water. Nicole and Elyse — I assume you started with the ferret?"

"What's your point?" Nicole asked.

"Kenneth, Miriam, and I found the cage of mice, right by our room. And lastly ..."

"What?" Deborah asked as Tyler turned to her.

"You knew that ferrets eat mice."

"So what?"

"Doesn't anyone think it's strange that we were in four groups, and pieces from all of us were required to keep that animal alive?" He ticked off fingers. "Mice. Water. Knowledge. And of course, the animal itself."

"Oh, for fuck's sake," said Elyse.

Tyler kept going. "It's starving and thirsty. It ran right up to the sink the second it got here. We had to work together."

"Bullshit." Ian sounded irritated, and maybe even pissed. "It's a fucking hairy rat. Who cares?"

"Maybe that's the question," Tyler said. "Are we the kind of beings who help other beings? Or the kind who only care about our own survival?"

"Even if you're right," Zach said, "Nobody *decided* whether or not to feed it."

"Deborah did."

"Well, bully for Deborah," said Elyse.

Miriam moved closer, almost as if she sensed pain and wanted to hug her. But Elyse shot her a look that kept her in place.

"That was luck, not teamwork," Kenneth said.

Tyler disagreed. "It wasn't. Doors had to open before we were together in the same room."

"Doors *we* didn't open," said Ian.

"*Luck*," Kenneth repeated.

"The doors opened when we made choices," Tyler insisted. "They didn't open at random."

"*They opened at random.*" Ian sat on a bunk, worrying his hands through close-shorn hair.

Tyler sat back, never comfortable with either the spotlight or confrontation. He had thoughts about everything, but they were ill-formed, needing data to fill them out.

"All right," said Zach, once the room was finally quiet. "Arguing won't solve anything. Tyler thinks we're being tested. Maybe that's true and maybe it's not. For *whatever* reason, the doors out there are opening and closing. But that's not all. I used to see a pink door through there. Now it's light blue."

"So the doors change color."

"Or the rooms are moving," Deborah suggested. "Can you feel the way the floor and walls keep shaking?"

"How the hell can *rooms move?*" asked Kenneth.

Then three things happened at once.

As if in response to his question, an orange door on the far side of the room opened ... just in time to show the frame shrinking in the shadow of advancing walls, the arch itself narrowing to reveal sliding gears and churning machinery. The floor trembled as the room slid past, rolling from one to another like chambers in a revolver.

Deborah, now clutching the ferret, screamed.

And Tyler, whose antennae were up, noticed the conspicuous absence of Marcus's voice. He should have been leaping in to take control as the game changed.

Tyler, and the others, turned toward Deborah, who

wasn't screaming at the moving room. She was screaming at Marcus, who was halfway through the used-to-be-black door, holding that little card he'd taken from the pile of papers. He was staring at it, advancing backward, trying to escape unseen. His eyes widened as they fixed on the card, a look of horror dawning on his face.

His mouth opened — maybe to explain why he was trying to sneak out like a coward or to voice his deadly realization. Maybe to argue.

But Deborah wasn't screaming about his attempted escape. She was crying out at a growing green light, hovering mid-air above his head, about the size of a golf ball, growing larger and throbbing with menace.

Very carefully, Miriam took a step toward Marcus. Hands up and out.

"Come toward me, Marcus. Nice and slow."

But the ball of light became a beam, then a column enveloped him same as the mouse.

An ozone plume blew outward, momentarily everywhere like a zero-gravity fire.

Then Marcus was gone, leaving flaming scraps of cloth to dance in the air, the card he'd been holding slowly seesawing downward, a wave of burning stench wafting on the breeze.

The alien clock ticked on.

Chunk.

Chunk.

One door opened.

Another closed.

The room beyond the red door jerked then moved upward, soon to be replaced by another.

8

EVENTUALLY THE ROOMS stopped moving and the doors stopped opening and closing. The machine around them reached stasis in what looked, to those who dared to venture out and peek, to be an entirely different configuration than the one they had come through earlier.

Even though most of the rooms looked alike, the colors had changed. Everything had shuffled, cut off, opened up, and tightened like a vice around them. They were a box of rocks, shaken and randomized — aware now there wasn't just left and right, but up and down, as well.

Hours passed. Food appeared through a slot in the kitchen. Fruit and nuts in many combinations. Miriam sat on a bunk, knees to her chest, eating what she could to keep her strength, doing her best not to look like a basket-case. She tried to smile and help, but folded inward when no one needed her. She barely spoke, and inside her walls continued to crumble. Everyone was afraid. But Miriam, with her proclivity, was more scared than most.

She felt trapped in this strange place. But three times now, she'd felt it squeeze tight enough that she had to clench her fists and wait for breath. It was the deepening of a horror she'd somehow grown used to, moved from uncomfortable to intolerable.

Miriam suffered from claustrophobia but could usually keep the fear at bay by distracting her mind. In elevators, she thought about the people she was on her way to see. In a crowd, she focused on whatever held its attention. Her city, Holiday Bend, was small. She'd never been mobbed. There'd been a bit after the outbreak, of course, but everyone had quickly forgotten then left her corner of the planet alone. That had been before the Astrals, back when the world was crazy but not yet insane.

What if someone locked all the doors?

When focused on restricted movement, Miriam verged on panic.

The plane probably won't go down ... but what if I just really, really want fresh air and can't get out?

On her honeymoon, her husband Bernard talked her into caving, promising large caverns and high roofs free of bats. The guide led them on a slippery slope, nudging Miriam into smaller and smaller slots. She'd had a full-blown panic attack in a pitch-black chamber they'd only reached by crawling on their bellies. A medic needed to deliver tranquilizers before she could calm herself enough to safely climb out. That night, so soon after tying the knot, Bernard slept on the couch.

So far, she'd kept herself distracted in this odd place, in the best way she knew — by trying to help those around her. In the first room, Kenneth and Tyler hadn't wanted her help, but she'd offered it anyway. That worked until they'd been shut in the tiny chamber with the mice and her panic returned.

That was the first time it'd been near-suffocating in here.

For moments, after trading the small chamber for Zach and Ian's larger room, Miriam felt better. But immediately thereafter, Nicole and Elyse started to bang from across the room, and her fear and empathy blended, her mind transporting her into the closed-off place — trapped all over again.

She'd looked around the room for a distraction, then saw the map. She'd noticed it in the other room, and how similar it looked to an aerial of her own town, as distributed by the USGS, as forwarded by the feds as part of an epidemic prep kit in the wake of the Phineas flu outbreak.

Barricade locations, checkpoints from which police would keep citizens — and the flu — from spreading. Walls, meant to close in an entire town.

Her fear had spiked. It was better after the second room opened, and all nine of them came together.

Well, eight now.

But it'd been a long time full of stillness. Three or four hours since Marcus had been disintegrated, if Miriam had to guess (though their timepieces had stopped working). Now, she had nothing left to distract her. Nothing but her claustrophobic thoughts. The alien clock kept time with her heartbeat, two rhythms in ominous sync. She watched, wondering. The others seemed to think it was counting down, and maybe it was. But what if it only told the time, to account for their broken watches? What if it was counting *up*?

BREATHE, Miriam. In ... then out.

It didn't help. Her mind kept returning to the quarantine.

No matter where she tried to focus, her eyes kept finding the map. She recalled that old, almost-forgotten feeling of disquiet. Remembered what it'd been like, years ago. The order to trap her constituents inside her town with an enemy no one could see. The flu mutated inside Holiday Bend, or so said the guys and gals at the top. That meant those who weren't already on their way out of town needed to stay *in* town. She'd been traveling on business, but her family had almost been locked inside.

Almost.

Miriam had thought of it often.

What if her husband and children had never left Holiday Bend? Many didn't. Phineas killed three percent worldwide but took her town to the tune of 20.6. Statistically, if they'd stayed, every member of her family would have faced a one-in-five chance of dying — odds worse than Russian roulette. It could have taken them. One easily, maybe all four. And what if Miriam, as mayor, had given the order that trapped them there to die?

Thank God they'd gotten out, just in time.

She wondered if the new *they* — Kenneth, Nicole, Elyse, Tyler, Ian, Deborah, Zach, and herself — would be able to do the same.

"Will you put that *down?*" Nicole told Ian.

He was holding the card that had so captivated Marcus, made him obsessed and unwilling to let it go, before the green light took him. The thing was a bit singed. They'd all taken looks, just in case. In the hours since, some of the room's artifacts began to seem familiar. The card certainly hadn't seemed random to Marcus.

Ian frowned, staring, subtly shaking his head.

Familiar. Again, Miriam's gaze found the map. *Yes, some of this is definitely familiar.*

She hadn't told anyone about the map. But fair was fair. They hadn't yet discussed Elyse and the bear she wouldn't put down — the one she claimed was her nephew's.

Elyse wasn't the only one with a connection to something here. Tyler kept futzing with the whiteboard. Kenneth said he'd used the exact same book of swatches while remodeling his hospital, and everyone felt the photo of the dirty people behind a fence rung a bell — all but Ian, who'd gone from recognizing it to denying he'd ever seen it. The ferret was curious, as well. It stuck closest to Nicole, who hated the animal, but Elyse mentioned she'd named it after a friend's ferret. Who owned a ferret? Wasn't that a coincidence?

Familiar.

Yes. That's what this was. Unnervingly so.

"I feel like I know this name," Ian said, meaning the name on the card. He paid Nicole's irritation no mind. They'd all been on-edge, but Nicole was fit to burst. More than anyone, she kept trying to find answers and coming up dry. Miriam, who'd spent years in therapy, had an armchair diagnosis. The woman was ruffling her feathers so she wouldn't seem as terrified and helpless as she felt. *Overcompensation*, they called that — like when a man with a little dick bought a big car.

"*Pryia Patel,*" Ian recited. "Seriously … nobody else recognizes it?"

No one answered. Ian kept asking the same question.

"Tyler? Do *you* know a Priya Patel?"

"Why would *I* know?"

"Her card says she works for Gladmoor Diagnostics. They had an exclusive contract as peer review for the CDC. You work for the CDC."

"It's a big organization."

"So you *don't* know her?"

"I said I didn't."

"But are you telling the truth?"

Tyler seemed about to respond to Ian's accusation when Elyse piped up.

"How about *you*, Ian? How is it that you know about some random lab's affiliation with the CDC?"

"I produced a lot of pieces about pH₁N₁ during the outbreak," Ian said, defensive. "You learn things."

"Uh-huh. I remember your 'pieces.'"

Elyse's tone made Miriam sit up. "What's that supposed to mean?"

"Nothing. Just ... *Overlook.*"

Deborah snickered. She was uncharacteristically still, eating peanuts. Kenneth told her to keep them far away from him. It'd be cruel and unusual to die of anaphylactic shock before alien annihilation.

"What?" Zach asked.

"Oh, please," said Elyse. "You of all people know what it means to be in bed with Overlook Media."

"What the hell?" Zach said, affronted by the sudden rain of shrapnel. "What did I do?"

"Your boss is practically *fucking* Randolph Hays. Overlook's 'news' is the reason he got elected."

"You mean the president?"

Elyse rolled her eyes. Miriam thought Zach might snap back, but he struck her as little more than a doormat.

Ian took up the cause instead. "Maybe keep your opinions to yourself."

Elyse laughed.

"Who asked you, anyway?" Ian asked.

"It's my job," she said, dark bangs like curtains across her forehead. "You know. Journalist to 'journalist.'"

The audible quotes around her second *journalist* made Ian stand. Kenneth, too, roughly between them, his body language more bouncer than co-captive. Elyse laughed harder.

Ian sat back down. "You're not a journalist."

"More than Overlook. You're not news. You're a propaganda machine."

"Easy," said Kenneth.

"When's the last time *you* broke a big story, Elyse? And by the way, I missed your latest show. How did that 'hard-hitting interview series' with alien abductees turn out? I was riveted. Did the old grandmother go back to her knitting? How about the guy with the lazy eye? *Did* someone feed his cats while he was away?"

"Oh, fuck off."

"Seriously. Everyone?" Ian stood again, now grand-standing for the others. "You've never seen anything as hard-hitting as Elyse's show! You miss it, you're neglecting your civil duty as an American. And ... hey ... wasn't *Wake Up!* the force behind that miracle cure, Delilah Root? You *grilled* the guy who sold that shit. I mean ... he ground up some fucking plant and it fucking *cured the flu,* just like that. I'm so glad you broke the story over coffee and scones while your 'co-hosts' sat around laughing at celebrity antics. Oh, and you know who else is grateful? *Tyler.* Right, Tyler? You guys didn't have to do *anything* after everyone started taking Delilah Root instead of ... you know ... the official vaccine. *Right?*"

Instead of fighting back, Elyse hugged the teddy bear. Tyler hadn't risen to Ian's bait, but Miriam saw him studying Elyse now, noting the strange way Ian's cheap shot about the bogus herbal cure had silenced her when she'd been raring to fight only moments before.

"Take it easy," Zach said.

"Oh, good," Nicole scoffed. "The president's errand boy has finally come to the rescue."

"Shut the fuck up, Nicole," Zach snapped.

Nicole looked over at him, shocked. "Wait. So you *do* have testicles?"

"Everyone just calm down," Kenneth said.

"I'm calm. I'm *always* calm. The rest of you have a problem? Fine. Deal however the hell you want. As for me, I've about fucking had it." Ian marched toward the closest open door.

Miriam had lost her bearings since the door-shuffling earlier, but she thought it might have been the black one.

"Don't go out there," said Kenneth.

"*Eat it,* Boy Scout."

Her fog lifted, the pieces starting to come together. Miriam caught Tyler's gaze. Judging by appearances, he had a revelation of his own.

The pictures on the wall.

The items in the room.

All of us, unrelated.

But it isn't random at all.

"*Ian!*" Tyler barked, shooting looks between Ian and Miriam.

"What?"

"That photo." Tyler pointed at the framed poster. "What do you know about it?"

"What the hell are you talking about?"

"I swear, I think I've seen it on TV. And in print. In all forms of ... of *media.*"

Media.

Then Miriam got that part, too.

Media.

Overlook Media.

She'd watched the TV spots and read the articles — anything to broaden her horizons and distract her mind after she'd ordered the quarantine.

Miriam remembered running across Overlook's propaganda and thinking, *Why was the CDC so convinced the flu had hybridized in contaminated chicken eggs, then spread in the hamlet of Holiday Bend, Wisconsin?*

According to Ian's company, none of that was important. In truth, it'd been brought into the country by immigrants. Spread by immigrants. It was all the immigrants' fault.

And in those ads was the photo displayed in every room of this obscene alien puzzle.

Tyler stood. He moved directly to the whiteboard, pointed at a mess of numbers and letters, and announced, *"It's all my fault. I made a mistake!"*

He looked up. Around.

Then he ran for the door opposite the one Ian seemed ready to stalk through, gunning hard until a ball of green light grew behind him.

It swelled.

Fired a beam of light.

After that, Tyler was no more.

9

ZACH WATCHED KENNETH PACE, stopping again to study the whiteboard. The man couldn't sit still. Or let anything go.

"Forget it," said Deborah.

Kenneth looked up at her.

"Why?"

"Are you a mathematician?"

"No."

"So," she said, waving at the incomprehensible mess of formulae, "forget it."

"Tyler wasn't a mathematician."

"Are you a specialist in infectious diseases?"

"No, but I work in a hospital."

"So what? I'm closer to being able to get this than some administrator, and I don't understand the equations at all. No offense."

Kenneth thought about arguing, but Deborah was right. He *was* an administrator; she *was* more in Tyler's line of work than him. Nobody had a clue, and they'd been arguing about what Tyler had done for the past hour or two —

enough time that their unseen hosts had delivered another meal. More fruit and nuts.

Kenneth returned to a bunk. The doors were still open. The rooms hadn't moved. If Tyler hadn't been zapped on his way out, he'd have had a straight shot to ... well, to whatever unknown crap they might head into now. "I'm starving."

"Then eat." Deborah, more than anyone, had taken to studying the room. Everyone was afraid to leave it — that's the mistake Tyler and maybe even Marcus had made — but its contents were apparently fair game.

"I'm allergic to peanuts," he said.

"Eat the fruit."

"It might have peanut dust on it."

"Wash it off, then."

"I'm *very, very* allergic," Kenneth said.

In the quiet, Nicole stood. "We should explore."

"I'm exploring," Kenneth answered.

"I meant the other rooms."

"And get fried? No thanks."

Nicole said, "Why so many rooms, if they don't want us to move around?"

"Lady? I hope you're not suggesting 'moral intention' or whatever. Because that was a theory most popularly expounded by our good friend Tyler." Elyse pointed at a scorch mark on the ground.

"Show some respect," Ian said.

"Sarcasm is my coping mechanism."

"Really?" Kenneth looked over. "I thought it was that bear."

Elyse held it tighter. Zach wanted to ask about it, but they'd done that with zero results already.

"We need to find a way out," Nicole said. "We won't find it sitting here. We explored before and nothing happened."

"Tyler was running for the door," Ian said.

"He also announced that it was *all his fault.*"

Nicole didn't need to elaborate. They'd beaten the issue to death, and nobody had any idea *what*, if anything, was Tyler's fault. He said he'd made a mistake, indicating the board. Unfortunately, nobody knew what the numbers meant. "My fault" might mean the reason they were all inside the big metal maze, but there was no context or way to be sure of what he had confessed to.

"So?" said Deborah.

"They killed him because of whatever he did, not because he was trying to leave the room."

"You don't know that."

"Neither do you."

Deborah shrugged.

"Look," Nicole said. "We can't just sit here."

Kenneth looked at her. "That's exactly what we're going to do."

Ignoring him, Nicole addressed Deborah. "We heard you in the maze. You were all over the place, weren't you?"

"Me and Marcus." Her gaze darted to the other scorch mark.

"You said there were patterns in the rooms."

"Just that they weren't in a straight line. They were in a gentle spiral, which led us here, to the center."

"We won't know this is the center unless we go out and look around. If it's a spiral, there must be an outer edge. Spirals aren't circles, which are closed."

"You got a point?" Kenneth asked.

"Just that I'm not willing to wait here and see what happens when that big clock thing reaches zero ... or whatever it's headed toward. I'd think you of all people would feel the same, Kenneth."

"Why me?"

"Because you can't eat what they give us. Or do you want to starve?"

Kenneth looked at the door. Nothing was moving now, but that could change. "It's not even the same layout as before. It could change once we leave."

"If we stay here, we're trapped for sure."

"We'll get lost. Not be able to find each other again."

"There are ropes," said Nicole, indicating the pile that looked like something from a ship's hold.

"You're kidding."

Nicole went to the stash, grabbed a heavy line, then headed toward Elyse.

"Not even a little," said Elyse.

"Miriam?"

She'd had a strange look in her eye ever since the thing with Tyler. Now Miriam stared at Nicole.

"You, then, Zach."

"Why me?"

"Because nobody else is brave enough."

Clearly bullshit. Zach tried to laugh but couldn't manage it.

Nicole still held the coil of rope.

"Why don't you go, Nicole?" Miriam asked.

"Excuse me?"

"It was your idea. You go, if you're so hot on it."

"I have the plan," Nicole said.

"Really? Okay. What is it."

"I told you. We need to explore. Find the exit."

"What if there is no exit?"

"Then we'll be no better off than we are right now."

Still she held the line for Zach.

Miriam said, "What's 319?"

Nicole looked back at her. "Excuse me?"

"Tyler said it was his fault," Miriam answered. "The mistake? What did he do wrong?"

"We already covered that," Nicole said.

Zach reached for the rope.

"Don't," Miriam said.

Zach stopped.

"How old was he, Elyse?"

The whole room looked from Miriam, whose strange demeanor had been holding their attention, to Elyse.

"Excuse me?" Elyse asked.

Miriam said, "How old was your nephew when he died?"

Elyse looked like she'd been tripped. She sat back further, knees up tighter, holding the bear closer. She looked less like the TV personality Zach knew her to be, and more like a teenage girl in crisis.

"What?"

"How old, Elyse?"

Nobody spoke. Until Elyse said, "Nine."

Whispers.

"How ... How did ...?" Ian began.

"Again, Zach." Miriam turned toward him. "What does 319 mean? I've seen the way you keep stealing glances at the skull over there. I saw the way your eyes widened when you looked into the next rooms and saw the same skull there, too. I'm tired. I tell the truth, and hate being lied to. So, tell me. Why are you so interested in that skull?"

"It's just interesting."

"You're lying." Kenneth, weighing in. "I've seen it, too."

Ian leaned forward. "You know something about why we're here, Zach?"

"No."

"Come on," said Deborah. "You talk to the president. You're his guy."

"I'm Health and Human Services, not CIA. Not NSA. Nobody tells me secrets."

"Really," said Ian.

Zach tried to evade, but all eyes were on him. "It just reminds me of something at work."

"What?" Kenneth moved forward, threatening.

Miriam said, "He's not to blame. Tyler was to blame, remember?"

"Tyler was trying to make a run for it," said Nicole.

"Where?" Miriam asked. "Tyler was watching everything from the moment I woke up. He just took it all in. He looked at the skull, too. And the poster Ian used to make immigration a scapegoat."

Kenneth and Nicole looked from Ian to the poster then back.

Zach recognized the image, of course. His boss, the president, was far-right on immigration. The administration hadn't thought to blame the plague on newcomers, but was pleased when Overlook Media had.

Miriam continued. "Tyler wasn't running. I don't know why he said what he said or what it meant, but he wasn't dumb enough to think he could just bulldoze his way through that maze of shifting rooms. He *realized* something."

"What?" Kenneth asked.

"I don't know. But he said it when Ian threatened to leave."

"Ian leaving made him think of something?"

Zach had been a science major before switching to politics. He knew all about making a hypothesis, then testing it. That's what Tyler's spike of inspiration sounded like to him.

But what theory had he been testing?

"Tyler said that whoever's keeping us in here had a sense of what they wanted versus what they didn't want to see from us," Miriam said. "That there's a right and wrong."

"And that they were testing us, not just watching," added Elyse.

Miriam looked around. "Go through the maze if you want. But the answers are here in this room."

"Or in all of them," Kenneth suggested.

"The rooms are the same," said Zach.

"Not exactly." Deborah moved to one door and then the other.

"Kenneth," Miriam said. "You said you recognized that book of paint swatches. You were ... what ... repainting your hospital?"

"A wing, yes. But it was years ago. I only remember the book because it has a funny brand name."

"What does your hospital do? Is there a specialty?"

"It's only a hospital."

"But it's near me. Near that town." Miriam pointed at the map.

Zach looked. "That's your town?"

"Yes. Holiday Bend. I'm the mayor. We already know Kenneth's hospital is nearby."

"But I'm in DC. Tyler was in Atlanta."

"Working for the CDC. Look closer at that map." Miriam pointed again. "Do you see the lines drawn over the roads leading in and out of town?"

Kenneth was first, inspecting. "What's your point?"

"Deborah. What do you do?"

"I work for Wotring Supply."

"What does Wotring do?"

"We make ventilators and masks."

"For firefighters?" Elyse asked. "Or for Halloween?"

"Mostly N-95 respirators." When nobody reacted, she said, "You know. Medical masks."

"And Kenneth runs a hospital," Deborah said. "You're saying they're connected?"

Kenneth shook his head. "We don't use them as a matter of course."

"'As a matter of course,'" Miriam repeated. Then she waited.

"Well, we use them during outbreaks."

"Like a flu outbreak?"

Inhales around the room. Now it was settling in.

"There's a reason we're all here together. Something we have in common. Tyler was working it out, and I've been doing the same. We're all different. Not a lot in common. Other than the fact that we're all Americans, I'd say we have nothing obvious in common at all. Except ..."

Except the flu, Zach thought.

"That map is identical to one that landed on my desk when the Phineas flu outbreak hit." Miriam glanced at the map. "It was part of a quarantine packet from the CDC."

She looked at the scorch where Tyler, of the CDC, had made his last stand.

"Kenneth, your hospital would've gotten a lot of our flu patients. Ian, your company ran those scare ads, featuring *that* image" — she pointed — "during the outbreak. Deborah works for a company that makes ventilator masks for outbreaks, like the flu. Marcus ..." Miriam made a face. "Him, I'm not sure of."

Ian cleared his throat. "Priya Patel. I remember why I knew the name. She works for an oversight lab because she's a do-gooder. Her lab supposedly keeps an eye on the CDC as well as the virus market, but she came off to me like a whistleblower."

"Came off when?" Kenneth asked. "How?"

"One of my guys interviewed her. It was red-hot, full of great gossip. I only heard about it ... before someone buried it."

"Who?"

"I don't know. Someone further up the chain than me."

"Why? What was in it?"

"Do you remember NuFaze?"

Heads nodded.

Kenneth said, "Anti-viral drug, right? But it was never really distributed to us, which was—"

"Strange, considering that Miriam's town was suppos-edly the epicenter?" Ian said. "I sure thought so. I didn't connect it all until later. That was a crazy time, with all the people dying. But what Ms. Patel alleged was that NuFaze didn't actually help anyone. She said it actually made people *more* susceptible to the killer flu."

"It passed the FDA, though," Kenneth said.

"Yeah. And do you know what else I remember about Priya Patel? She was liaison to the FDA."

Nicole said, "Marcus was staring hard at the card when he was shot with the beam. And when we were alone, just the two of us, he said something about working for the government. In Silver Spring, Maryland."

"And?"

"I grew up fifteen miles from Silver Spring. It's where the FDA is headquartered."

Murmurs. Heads turning.

Kenneth's face turned to disgust. "He lied. I'll bet that's what it was. He let NuFaze through approval, and instead of helping people survive the flu, it helped them die."

"You don't know that," said Zach.

"And besides," Deborah added, "Tyler said, 'It was my fault.'"

"Him too, then," Kenneth said. "They covered it up together."

"Oh, bullshit." Zach shook his head. "Believe it or not, the government isn't always covering things up."

"Really? Okay, Zach. What's '319' mean?"

Zach breathed once, twice.

"It's just a coincidence."

"What's it mean, Zach?" Miriam pressed.

"There's a section in the Public Health Act. Section 319."

"And what's it do?"

"In the event of an emergency, we can invoke Section 319 to waive Medicare/Medicaid requirements so low-income patients can seek medical care."

"Think Tyler would know that?"

"Probably not by number, but it affects him, too. The Section's main purpose isn't necessarily to save lives—"

"Of course it isn't," Kenneth said, arms crossed.

Zach went on with a hard stare at Kenneth. "It's to prevent the spread of disease. It crosses CDC and H&HS, with both being impacted."

"And you ... what ... invoked it for the Phineas flu?"

Zach waited. Breathed once, twice.

"Yes. But we waited too long. The president ... Shit ..."

"Come on, Zach," said Kenneth. "Why stop now?"

"The president threatened to fire me if I invoked it when the CDC made us aware we should. He was concerned about the budget. It was fragile at the time, and a big point in his re-election campaign the following year."

"So he let all the poor people die to win an election," Kenneth said. "Or rather, *you* did. Just like Marcus probably did. Just like Tyler, apparently, did."

"Three government officials," said Ian. "Three liars. What are the chances?"

Zach felt something crumbling. He'd known, of course. He'd known all along. He could have fought to invoke Section 319. His successor, if Zach was fired, could have fought even harder. The Section would have been in place before the president knew it.

He could have saved lives.

But he didn't.

"Okay," he said, alarmed to find himself nearing tears. "Fine. I admit it. I should have—"

There was a flash of light, and then Zach saw no more.

10

KENNETH HAD them all lined up. Like an inquisition.

It was the next morning, if there was such a thing. There were still six people in the room. Nobody had vanished. The room seemed unchanged, but the rooms around them were different. At some point in the night, six additional doors had opened, making a total of eight. Beyond each was a room like the one that everyone other than Ian and Zach had woken in. Smaller, no kitchen, no water, two doors on opposite walls and a colored door that, in this case, opened into the large central room they reluctantly called home.

At first, the openings seemed like a curiosity, revealing rooms they'd already known were there just beyond the doors. But then a ninth one opened, and beyond that was nothing. Darkness with no bottom or top — not even sides where the outer walls of the adjacent rooms should have been.

Deborah, the boldest, grabbed the frame and leaned out, more fascinated than afraid. The others stayed back as if the black rectangle might bite them. Deborah said, "It's fine. It's okay," just as the alien ticking changed, the glyphs shifting shape, and the clock starting to double its pace.

"Double Jeopardy round," said Elyse.

Kenneth assumed it was supposed to be a dark joke. Nobody laughed.

Nor had anyone slept all the way through. A few tried. Kenneth knew the details. He'd taken a pencil and paper from the desk, interviewed each person, and recorded what they said. Nicole claimed to have been awake all night, trying to solve the room as if it were a riddle. Ian told him he'd woken twice and found Nicole sleeping once. She was lying, just like the others.

Food arrived. This time it was only peanuts.

"We're running out of time," Kenneth said.

"You mean, *you* are," said Elyse, moving too close to Kenneth, throwing peanuts down her throat.

He moved away and she came closer. His next step took him too close to the empty doorway — to the void. Kenneth smacked the wall near it with his shoulder. Elyse gave a smile somewhere between wicked and seductive, then retreated, legs back up, teddy bear in her lap.

"Take it easy, Elyse," said Miriam.

"Why? So I can be last? I'd rather die now, while I still have company."

"Knock it off," Ian snapped.

"Are you in charge now?" Elyse asked him.

"No. Kenneth is. Isn't that right, Kenny?"

Kenneth straightened his shirt, trying to regain some dignity. *Yes*, he was in charge. Nicole thought she was, and Deborah might think the same if she could settle down and stop fiddling with the room's artifacts like a dog chasing squirrels. But only Kenneth had the chops to organize people, the way he'd organized his hospital.

Armed with what they'd learned before Zach had been zapped, Kenneth spent much of his evening and night chasing clues. He started with the business card — and yes, the name was still Priya Patel, still with the watchdog lab, her second-hand story still jibing with Ian's narrative, once Kenneth finished his interrogation.

According to Ian, Patel's lab discovered a fault in the anti-flu drug but Marcus seemed to have pushed it through, anyway. Well-intentioned, perhaps. But he'd aided the deadly virus nonetheless.

It all came back to the flu.

Overnight, Kenneth examined the whiteboard. But he didn't know the math. Same for the mechanics and metrics the CDC used to track the spread of disease. He did know what Tyler confessed.

It was his fault, he'd made a mistake.

It implied that somewhere on the board lay an incorrect equation.

Tyler must have gotten his digits wrong somewhere, miscalculating the spread. Because he'd used the word *fault*, Kenneth inferred that Tyler's mistake might have been honest, but that his actions thereafter were not. Like Marcus, he must have covered something up, also aiding the flu. Just as Zach, by failing to enact Section 319 and keep the poor both medicated and close to home, made it easier for the flu to spread.

Now Kenneth had them all lined up. All on trial, himself included.

Elyse — after her half-threat, half-insanity— was back in place. Catatonic, with that bear again, apparently responsible for hawking that bullshit herbal cure the world had heard about from her very own talk show. Delilah Root, which the inventor claimed could protect people from the flu better than vaccines — seeing as they were in too-short supply and a vaccine snafu might have started it all in the first place.

That much, he'd confirmed with Ian as well. Overlook Media might be a tribe of fear-mongering, reactionary fuckers, but they did their homework. They knew about Priya Patel's warning to the FDA, which Zach had ignored, and they knew why pHiNi had gone so very bad in the years before the Astral occupation.

Going down the line, all suspects reporting in.

Kenneth himself ran a hospital, Mercy Medical. Given its proximity to Holiday Bend, it was no surprise Mercy was overrun. He remembered the epidemic well, and knew — if this really was all about the flu — why he was here. Mercy, in the strictest sense, had failed. They'd fallen short on ventilators, N-95 masks like the ones Deborah's company made, special medications, and vaccine to treat the uninfected. But that wasn't his fault. Kenneth was a master of budget, but his forecast hadn't foreseen the coming crisis. Check one for the good guys.

Miriam, they already knew, was mayor of Holiday Bend — the city where the outbreak supposedly started. From what Kenneth could both tell and remember, Miriam had done her job. She'd enacted the quarantine; she'd shut the city's borders to contain the spread. Another person whose presence made sense, but score a second point for the good guys as well.

Elyse, they all knew, had signed Delilah Root as a sponsor for her daytime talk show, *Wake Up!* Her nephew extracted overnight and died of the flu. Hence her attachment to the bear. But why, assuming the Astrals stocked this place as a test, had they put that particular totem in play? What did it mean?

In Kenneth's mind, Elyse was both guilty and innocent. She'd taken the sponsor, and was paid to do so. The world, desperate with the dying and short on legitimate vaccine after the first batch went bad, was looking for another solution. But had Elyse known Delilah Root did nothing? Kenneth wasn't sure.

Ian produced scare campaigns, blaming immigration for the flu's wildfire spread. According to Overlook's many news programs, immigrants were to blame. What must that have done? Kenneth, from his career in healthcare, thought he knew. Immigrants wouldn't go in for treatment as the world turned against them. They'd hide, run, do what illegals always did when avoiding persecution. It wouldn't have corralled the disease. It would have spread it faster. One point for the bad guys, perhaps.

That left Deborah, whose company made N-95 masks needed by outfits like the Red Cross to safely treat the disease, and Nicole, who wouldn't say a damn thing. Under different circumstances, if he had been a different kind of person, Kenneth might have beaten it out of her. Ironically, the only one among them who seemed capable of beating a confession out of anyone was Nicole herself. She appeared to have the ambition, if it promised to clear her name.

Kenneth paraded in front of them, drawing looks of ire from Miriam, Elyse, and Nicole. Ian was in his own world, and Deborah was too excited about solving the puzzle — even if the reward was death — to care.

They could hate him, but Kenneth intended to see tomorrow.

"You realize," he told Nicole, "that refusing to say anything makes us assume you did something wrong."

"Sue me," she said.

"Tyler said this is a puzzle the Astrals are using to test us, just like they tested Austin with that bomb cube they dropped, just like they peep into people's minds with those lines of stones. I'm inclined to agree. I don't care what you did, but I do care about passing this test. We'll die if we don't solve the puzzle."

"News for you, Kenny," said Elyse, dour. "If you *do* solve the puzzle, you die, too."

"We don't know that."

"Sure we do. Marcus was staring at that business card, realizing that his rushing NuFaze through FDA approval despite the warnings killed people, when he was zapped. Zach was in the middle of admitting his failure when they got him. And Tyler?" Nicole laughed. "He spread his arms and announced it to the world."

He had, hadn't he? Kenneth was good at organization, not as good at deduction. People like Tyler — and in research, he'd known a few — always felt ten steps ahead. It was strange that Tyler made such a decisive mistake. He hadn't been found out. He'd turned himself in. Why, if he was so smart?

"Let's say something I did, in some way, contributed to the spread of pHiNi that year. What possible incentive could I have for telling you about it?"

"The more we know, the closer we'll be to solving this thing."

"And the closer I'd be to dead," Nicole said. "If I had a part in this. Which I did not."

Kenneth pondered. Yes, that was a problem. For all of them.

He looked around the room, stopping at Miriam.

"You said there were objects in the room. Something with meaning for each of us."

Miriam nodded, her mood darkened.

"I have the book of paint colors I used to paint my hospital wing. Elyse has the bear. You have the map of Holiday Bend. Tyler had the whiteboard. Ian ..." Kenneth scratched his head. "I guess the photo is yours. Did you choose it, for use in Overlook's ads?"

"Maybe, or maybe not," said Ian, taking Nicole's hint.

"Zach had the skull. Marcus ... the business card. Deborah ... *hmm*. What sticks out for you?"

She shrugged. "I don't know."

"I've looked through everything. There's—"

A noise came from one of the newly-opened rooms. Deborah, acting rather than thinking, as seemed her habit, rushed through the door.

She gasped.

Forgetting themselves, the others followed. Kenneth, too, before he thought better of it.

Looking out the doors of the second-level room, they saw nothing. Where there'd once been a maze, now there was only blackness.

"It's spreading," Deborah said.

A flash of green light emanated from the main room, which they all had abandoned to look.

Except for Elyse.

She was gone when they returned, leaving only the bear and a note right beside it.

11

ELYSE'S NOTE READ:

I KNEW Delilah Root was useless.

I pushed it anyway, for money. Anti-vaxxers wanted to believe in a cure that didn't involve pharma. So I gave it to them.

I pulled it when my nephew died.

He didn't stand a chance because of me.

I'm sorry.

If there's a Hell, I'll see you there.

DEBORAH SET IT DOWN. Kenneth and Miriam read the note over her shoulder. Ian and Nicole hadn't, and were fighting over it now. Deborah didn't want to hold the paper one second longer. Guilt bled onto the page, burning her hand. She'd seen Elyse scribbling. Realizing, in retrospect, that she'd seen a suicide note being written gave Deborah a chill.

"So that's that," said Ian, setting down the note.

"That's that?" Deborah could feel the ferret at her feet.

Morpheus, the sixth uncredited member of their dwindling group.

"She knew it didn't work. She's as guilty as the rest of them."

"By 'the rest of them,'" Nicole said to Ian, "do you mean Zach, Tyler, and Marcus?"

"Yes."

"They were guilty, and so was Elyse?"

"Of course." Ian looked from Nicole to Deborah, both of whom were staring at him. "What?"

But Deborah knew what Nicole was saying. If the dead's actions, combined, had caused the Phineas outbreak and resulted in three percent of the population dying, it meant the aliens had known — had judged them right by bringing them here.

What did it say about the remaining five?

Deborah's gaze went to the first aid kit, with its bright red cross. She'd investigated it when she'd cut herself on a bunk's sharp edge and found it empty. The case mattered, not the contents.

How many empties just like it had Deborah seen?

What should we do with them? her production manager had asked, as they looked out across the warehouse, at all those empty kits.

Deborah, back then, had no answer. She knew only that usually, kits like that would be stuffed with one of their N-95 masks and shipped off to the next station for the inclusion of bandages, more common cotton masks, ointments ... a hodge-podge with the minimum amateur and professional providers required to care for the sick, built through a geographically distributed assembly line.

What I don't understand, the manager had told Deborah,

is how we ran out of masks. We should have had more than enough to fill the orders.

Orders they would miss, Deborah had known. Orders she, in her entrepreneurial, hustler's excitement, had raffled off to the highest bidders. Rich people needed protection from the flu, so what did it matter if she broke protocol and sold them masks outside the loop? The supply chain would provide.

Except that it hadn't, because in her usual excitement to explore and break rules, Deborah forgot that even the Red Cross sourced from them, directly.

Store them, Deborah had said.

And they were stored so that they could clear the warehouse for when more masks were ready — a day that never came, while the aid organizations treated the ill unprotected and spread the disease.

But also so that Deborah, whose spectacular successes had always ironed out her failures, wouldn't need to look out across her warehouse and see only emptiness. Kits that couldn't save a single soul. Looking at those empty kits was like surveying a stack of corpses, stacked like human cordwood.

"Boom," someone said.

Ian.

Deborah snapped out of it, shoving the empty white kit with its red cross aside. Unlike the others' objects, hers was nondescript. The box could have been anything, even though to Deborah it was an accusing finger.

She looked at Ian. So did Kenneth, Miriam, and Nicole.

He was at the bunk where Nicole had been sleeping, holding something up. At first Deborah thought it was the business card, but on closer inspection she saw it was an ID. *Nicole's* ID.

"What the hell do you think you're doing?"

"Investigating," Ian said.

Nicole rushed forward. She'd been wearing a small designer waist pack but must have taken it off to sleep. Ian noticed and went snooping.

"Give me that."

"No," he said, *"Doctor."*

Nicole reached. Ian dodged.

"Doctor Nicole Davies," Ian read, holding it high like a game of keep-away.

"You're a doctor?" Kenneth asked.

"Goddammit, Ian! *GIVE ME MY PROPERTY!"*

Nicole leapt at him.

Ian pushed back, keeping his hand aloft. She slapped him.

With barely a pause, he hit her back. *Hard.*

Nicole fell to the floor, head racking the table leg.

She reached behind her head, and her fingers came away with blood. Everyone was looking at Ian.

"What?"

Nobody wanted to speak. Ian hadn't just pushed her away. That'd been a hit, one step down from a bar brawl punch. He hadn't closed his fist, but Nicole hadn't hitched. She'd gone sprawling with most of the force he could muster.

"She's hurt," said Kenneth, kneeling by Nicole.

"She's a doctor," Ian said. "She can fucking fix it herself."

Deborah took the ID. Nicole wasn't an M.D. She was a Ph.D. She owned a lab called First Line. Head scientist and CEO at a company with the tagline, *The frontier of virology.*

"Virology," Deborah said. "As in, the study of viruses."

"Someone want to grab some bandages?" Kenneth looked around. "I think I saw a first aid kit."

Miriam was already there. She'd popped the kit, suspiciously moved to Deborah's bunk rather than on the shelves, and was staring into its empty innards, confused.

"Did you hear me, Kenneth?" Deborah asked.

"I'm trying to help Nicole."

"Help *us* instead. Look at this!" Deborah jammed the ID into Kenneth's hand.

She didn't get angry often, but it was explosive when she did.

Deborah willed herself to calm, finally seeing the empty black doorway for the terrifying nothingness it was. Before now, in a way, the puzzle felt like a high-stakes game. Comfortable with risk, Deborah had been willing to play. Now she felt death's creeping finger. Three men were dead. Elyse had killed herself in despair, and Nicole, that cunt, had been hiding something important while looking down on the rest of them.

Kenneth watched Deborah's face before looking at the card. He saw the fire there, too.

Then he turned his eyes to the plastic in his hand.

"First Line?" He looked down at Nicole, still playing helpless on the floor. *"First Line* is your company?"

"I told you I owned a business." She sat up, apparently realizing the time for sympathy had passed.

"What's First Line?" Ian asked.

"It's one of the leading producers of flu vaccine," said Kenneth. "God knows I worked with them enough, trying to get enough supply."

Ian snapped his fingers, now pointing excitedly. "I know First Line! They ..." His face scrunched, assessing before saying something he wouldn't be able to take back. "The virus came from you."

"Attenuated virus," Nicole said, brushing herself off.

"But it mutated," Ian said.

"Hybridized," Nicole corrected. She tried to laugh, shaking her head. "You people. This is why I didn't tell you."

"Because you *started* it all? Because your fucking lab *created* the virus that killed millions of people?"

"Relax," said Nicole. "You don't understand."

"I understand plenty." Ian looked at the others. "Kenneth, back me up. You're a hospital guy. Viruses evolve quickly, and they crossed two of the streams. Contaminated eggs, wasn't it? And your QA people missed it when you injected it with the yearly strain."

"You're oversimplifying."

Ian was thinking, trying to remember his company's news reports. "There was a guy. A worker. He spilled something?"

"There was *contamination,*" Nicole said, clearly resenting the phase *spilled something*. "But we have protocols for that sort of thing. We think the flu started in a man named Watson Dufresne. He worked in one of our labs, but we contained him. It wasn't even the right line. It wasn't the flu that went public."

Ian wasn't buying it. Now that Nicole was up, he advanced on her. "Bullshit." He looked around at the others, then practically spit in her face and repeated it. "Bull*SHIT*. The aliens want someone to blame? Great. Let's end this right now." He shoved Nicole hard, almost making her trip. Then he jabbed a finger her way and shouted to nobody in particular. "*SHE* DID IT! *RIGHT THERE!*"

Nicole came forward again. Fearing a beam of green light, Deborah, Kenneth, and Miriam backed away.

But Ian met her in the middle, pushing harder.

She slammed into a desk's edge, rolled sideways, hit the wall.

And still he advanced.

"Stay away from me!" Nicole was trying to be self-important, but her veneer was cracking.

Deborah saw sheer terror beneath it. Ian was off the leash.

She moved away, lateral now, trying to stay out of Ian's grasp. Her eyes sought the others for help, but they were in the middle and not taking sides.

Ian got her by the shirt collar, face to face. Ravenous. Vengeful. She slapped at him but found no purchase.

He shook her like a rag doll and yelled into the air again. "You want someone to punish? Is this about the flu? We fuck up! Humans fuck up! A lot of people died, but you've got the ones who did it! If you care, fine! I didn't do anything! The others didn't do shit! But this one? This bitch right here?" She looked scrambled, fizzy like a dropped soda. Still he kept shaking her. "This is the bitch who started it!"

"Ian," Miriam said, "wait a minute. Just because Nicole—"

"SHE DID IT! ALL I DID WAS PLAY SOME POLITICS! I DIDN'T HURT ANYONE! I DIDN'T MEAN IT, BUT *SHE DID!* SO TAKE HER, AND LET ME THE FUCK OUT OF HERE!"

Deborah saw where Ian was going but couldn't react in time. The outer rooms shifted, and a second door opened into blackness across from the first. Two portals into nothing, with Ian marching Nicole to the first.

"*Ian!*" Kenneth shouted.

But he was there already, shoving her through, into the void.

In the same second, as if rejected from the belly of the cosmos itself, Nicole flew through the second door into blackness, across from the first. She spilled onto the floor as far from Ian as possible, having literally gone into nothing and back.

A warp corridor in their midst. Jump through one doorway and get thrown in from the second.

Ian looked at her and began to laugh. His mind was failing, his murder committed, yet not accomplished.

Now he looked lost.

With nobody to punish, his face fell.

And he said, "What? Why are you staring at me?"

It wasn't the obvious.

There was a green ball of light above his head.

All I did was play some politics.

Ian's admission. His guilt, in spreading the plague.

He looked up at the ball, his face gone slack. It grew. Pulsed. Swelled.

"Guys," he began.

But then Ian was gone.

12

THE CLOCK WAS the room's heartbeat. Beyond that, Miriam heard nothing.

At least, not until a massive grinding sounded, and two of the rooms with open doors moved laterally and away, leaving another pair of doorways with blackness behind them.

At first, they'd frightened Miriam because they were so inhuman, so vacant and impossible to understand. Now they terrified her because they were apparently less than nothing. Not ebony pits so much as folds in space — places where even from across the large room, disparate spots somehow touched.

Nicole proved it, having been thrown through one door only to fly back into the room from the other.

More grinding. Rooms moving through open doors. Now they were surrounded by what looked like empty space, but was really another side of everything. Look right, look left — see the same place.

It was hard for Miriam to wrap her head around, so she didn't try.

She sat.

The ferret, having lost his biggest fan, stuck close to Nicole, who clearly wanted nothing to do with it.

Watching, Kenneth said, "Ferrets."

Nicole replied, "There's only one."

"No. I mean, your company makes vaccines. They use ferrets in virology research. Right?"

Nicole stared into space. The room was in an odd detente. It wasn't lost on Nicole that Kenneth, Miriam, and Deborah, after Ian popped her secret, had done little to keep Ian from taking her. Miriam could only study her own reaction, but she supposed she'd wanted Ian to hurt her.

It went contrary to Miriam's nature, but she'd still let it go. In that moment, they'd all wanted someone to blame. A woman who'd hidden her rather important affiliation was perfect for the role.

But they were *all* to blame. Miriam had held off the quarantine order just long enough to let her family escape. Others — *infected* others — left Holiday Bend in that window of indecision. In the flu's post-mortem, she'd learned one of those flew home to New York, one to Pasadena, two to Europe, and one to China. Without Miriam — and without all the others sharing her room — the Phineas outbreak might have been a tenth as deadly.

And she, like Nicole, had kept her secret. She wasn't admitting it even now. Same as Nicole's justifications were likely a mile high.

Nicole was by herself, on the floor, not far from where Ian's throw had landed her. Miriam was on a bunk, not far but not at all close. Deborah and Kenneth were together, sitting on the same bunk. They'd formed a strange bond — opposites attracting, perhaps.

Miriam felt alone. Distant from the others, the vacuum between them triggered by guilt ... for a million transgressions, then and now.

"I think there are ferrets in the lab," Nicole admitted. "It's a big facility with a lot of people."

"That's barbaric," Deborah said.

"You'd rather we experiment on humans?"

"I'd rather you get it right."

Nicole's face scrunched. Now unmasked, she seemed a lot more talkative. Quiet kept her secret, but now she had pride to defend. The ferret crossed her ankles at the end of straight legs as she camped on the floor. She wiggled her leg to send it away — not quite a kick, but definitely a nudge.

"It wasn't our fault," she said.

"Your lab," said Kenneth. "Where was your quality control?"

"We knew we'd gotten a bad batch. Believe me, it didn't get past QA, regardless of what Overlook told the world. We have layers of checks in place, and I remember the report. Bird flu from bad chicken eggs, arriving in what were supposed to be sterile hard-shell incubators. *Of course* they were tested. Phineas was, yes, a hybrid of that flu and the annual candidate we were culturing to attenuate and use for vaccine. We don't exactly know how or where they crossed, but viruses are hearty and evolve quickly. I swear to you, on my life, we did not ship bad vaccine. Phineas got out *somehow*, but it was nothing we could have controlled."

"A sick worker?" said Deborah.

"We watched absences. All were quarantined. Even their homes were swept."

Quarantined. Miriam felt a chill.

"This is exactly why I didn't tell you. The news made us

look like the bad guy, but there's nothing we could have done."

Kenneth said. "I remember reading up. Your lab is in Oregon, but Patient Zero went through my hospital in Wisconsin."

"The hybridization happened at our Madison facility. Whatever escaped must have walked right out our back door."

Kenneth shifted, but it wasn't like he was going to rise and go after her. Nicole had already lived through one attempted murder today, and they were all bones in the end, anyway.

Deborah scanned the ceiling.

"What are you looking for?" Miriam asked.

"Green light."

"Why?"

"Because she confessed. When you admit guilt, they kill you."

"That didn't sound like a confession to me," Kenneth said.

"But we all know she's guilty, right?"

"Can you stop talking about me like I'm not here?" Nicole said.

Kenneth muttered, "Maybe if we wait a little, you won't be."

"That's not funny," said Miriam.

"It's a little funny." A light chuckle from Deborah.

But no green light.

"I don't understand," Deborah said.

"What?" Kenneth asked.

"She just admitted that her lab created the flu that killed all those people. So why—?"

"*Accidentally,*" Nicole said. "And however the virus

escaped, it was despite our best efforts."

"But the aliens seem to be punishing the people responsible for the Phineas outbreak. Part of that moral judgment Tyler was talking about."

That didn't sound right to Miriam. *Judging*, yes ... but *punishing?*

There had to be more to it than that. Knowledge clearly wasn't lacking.

The aliens already knew who each of them were, knew their respective roles in the outbreak's prodigious spread, and even knew symbols to put in the room for each responsible body. Nobody knew Miriam had dragged her feet on enacting quarantine other than Miriam — so how was there a quarantine map on the wall to remind her? There'd already been reports that the Astrals could read minds with their stones. According to Miriam's best guess, the objective truths here would only surprise the other human subjects. The Astrals already knew it all. If they'd wanted to punish them, why put the responsible parties in a room together?

What was the point? Why kill them off one at a time, rather than all at once?"

Miriam, scanning for a green beam that never came, settled on the bunk to her right. Elyse's bunk. The bear was still there. Miriam reached out and took it.

"Now *you're* going to carry it around?"

Miriam ignored Nicole and gently squeezed the toy. Elyse had been guilty from the start. She'd taken a sponsorship from that bogus herbal cure, then put its creator on a pedestal in front of the world. She'd done it for career and money — maybe even believing an herbal could work, perhaps deciding that *some* treatment was better than *no* treatment, seeing as the vaccine was in such short supply.

Maybe Elyse's intentions had been good, if selfish. She

hadn't known people would actively eschew the vaccine when it came available, opting instead for Delilah Root. But whether she'd known or not, the result wasn't any different. Sick people traveled and spread the disease, thinking they were well.

She'd regretted it in the end, when her nephew died of the flu, but how much difference could that make? The damage was done — a few more fleas escaping the bottle. No different from a nepotistic mayor who made quarantine exceptions for the people she loved.

Yet Elyse hadn't been killed until she'd written her note. She'd chosen the time of her passing.

Maybe you have to confess.

Her mouth opened, but Miriam said nothing.

"She was a bitch, anyway," said Nicole.

All eyes turned to her.

"I'm kidding."

"You're an asshole," Deborah said.

"To quote Elyse." Nicole made the air quotes. *"Sarcasm is how I cope."*

"You're thinking of denial. *Denial and deflecting blame* are how you cope."

Nicole shrugged as if to say *six of one, half a dozen of the other*.

Quiet descended. For a moment.

"She said I was a three," Nicole said.

"Who said that?"

"Elyse. That's why I said — why I joked — that she was a bitch. You people have no sense of humor."

"She ... What?"

"It was one of the first things she said to me. You know. *A three.* Out of ten." When nobody responded like she wanted, Nicole acted annoyed and said, *"As in I'm ugly."*

Miriam's forehead bunched as she mulled that over. That would be a strange thing for Elyse to say. Insulting someone you just met, especially on their looks and for no apparent reason, was a strange social choice. What's more, Nicole wasn't unattractive. She was beautiful — the kind of beauty that made Miriam jealous enough to hate herself for being so shallow. Miriam wasn't one to objectify, but if she had to, she'd rate Nicole an eight. At least.

Kenneth laughed. "I guess she didn't like you, either. She rated *Tyler* a five."

Deborah: "What?"

"Why was she rating anyone?" Miriam asked.

Then Deborah was snapping her fingers. Pointing excitedly.

"Oh. Oh! Did she 'rate' me? Did she say I was a seven?"

"Oh, fuck you," said Nicole.

"No, no. There's this thing. A personality test. This old partner of mine — he tested everyone he worked with. "The eggy ... edgy ..."

"Enneagram?" said Miriam. "Are you saying that Elyse was flagging people as Enneagram types?"

"What are you talking about?" Kenneth asked.

Deborah explained that Enneagram sevens like herself were excited, distractible, and "interested a million things but only one inch deep." But that exhausted her knowledge.

Miriam knew a little. Her friend Molly, who was a crystals and chakra type, bored her nearly to tears with it once. She wasn't remotely new age, but Miriam had listened to Molly's sermon on the ancient history and modern-day efficacy of the old personality types and agreed it sounded no worse a compass than Myers-Briggs.

Miriam remembered little herself, but did know there were nine types, each of which could slide into extremes of function or dysfunction depending on circumstance. Leader-types could be brave forces for change, for instance ... or tyrannical bullies.

Nine personality types.

Nine people gathered in a room.

It didn't sound like a coincidence.

"So what's a three?" Nicole asked.

"In-charge types," Kenneth answered. "Image conscious. Bold. Tendency toward arrogance."

"I thought you didn't know what it was?"

"I don't. I'm just reading you."

"I remember fives because they're in the middle," said Miriam. "Investigators. They analyze and assess. Sure sounds like Tyler."

Tyler, Miriam thought, *who'd figured something out ... then shouted his guilt and given up.* Something still felt wrong there. A chink in the armor of their collective theories.

"Deborah's a seven. If Tyler was a five and Nicole is a three, does that mean the rest of us comprised the other six?"

"That's a thin conclusion."

But Kenneth had been trying to pin people down — trying to nail accountability and separate right from wrong, imperfect from perfect — since the beginning. Miriam didn't know which number that was, but it wasn't three, seven, or five. Kenneth was different from the others like Miriam, who'd mostly been quiet and looked for ways to help.

Elyse with her brooding. Zach with his peacemaking, Marcus with his bold, intense manner. He was most like Nicole, but they remained distinct. Types overlapped, and one could shift toward the others in times of stress. From what her crystal-loving friend had said, the Enneagram was thousands of years old. Enough time for the Astrals, who'd apparently visited Earth, to know about.

Enough time, perhaps, that maybe they'd invented it — seeded it here on Earth.

"Thin or not," Miriam said, "it sort of fits."

"So what?" Nicole shrugged.

"Well, might that mean that this is a personality test as much as a morality test?"

"What, like they want to watch our group dynamics?" Deborah asked. "See when we work together? When we fight?"

"Maybe."

"To what end?"

"I don't know." Miriam's excitement was already starting to fade. The revelation — if that's what it was — had felt like a step toward understanding. And maybe it was, but she didn't know how.

If they're testing us, what do they hope to see?

The Astrals wouldn't have given them a puzzle if they weren't supposed to find a solution. This was a mystery begging to be solved, not a trial to endure. The Astrals, if they'd brought Miriam and the others together to lay blame, could have woken them on beds of burning-hot coals. Instead, they were given food, space, clues, and unknowns that begged for discovery.

The secrets each of them seemed to hold — their connections to the killer flu epidemic, and maybe their fault in making it one of modern history's worst — were tumblers in a lock. If there was no way to win, why had their captors asked them to play?

Miriam rubbed her head. She wasn't Tyler. She wasn't a five, to whom investigation came naturally.

"I don't see the point." Nicole shook her head.

Such a three thing to say.

Deborah sighed. "Look. I'm only my company's VP instead of its president because I have too many ideas and end up scattered. Running the business took a more focused mind, but it wouldn't exist if I hadn't formed it. I'm great at figuring things out, if I get interested in them. If we all think the way out is to understand why they brought us here, I'm all for it."

"Okay," said Kenneth.

"We each have a connection to the outbreak, right?" Deborah stood, then started to pace. "And I think it's fair to say that looked at through a certain lens, someone could lay blame on each of us for how bad it got — how far it spread before the world governments finally contained the problem. It shouldn't be surprising that the Astrals want to see how we handled a crisis, then take meaning from it later. They've laid those boulders everywhere, and I heard Delacroix saying that the lines might be like brain pathways. A massive neural network made of stone. It's like they're trying to understand us. Killing some of us, yes — but curious about how we think and act, as well."

"And?" Nicole asked.

Deborah had her hand to her chin, trying to focus. "Each of us has a clue. Each—"

"Except you. And me."

Deborah didn't look at Nicole, but she shook her head at Nicole's posit. "No, I have one. I just didn't say. It's that empty case that looks like a first aid kit."

"What does it mean? How do you know?" Kenneth asked.

Deborah made a face, thinking, dismissing. "No, I don't want to say. I'd rather not die. Not with this unfinished thought."

Miriam almost laughed, but it didn't seem to be a joke.

"Nicole." Deborah paced, pondered. "Right or wrong, fault or no fault, the virus started with you. With your Madison lab, not far from Miriam's town. Or Kenneth's hospital."

"I told you, we did everything we could to make sure—"

Deborah held out a hand, quieting her. "I know. I get it. I'm just thinking of the totem. What clue, in the room, is yours?"

"I have no idea."

Deborah leaned against a wall, as far from one of the empty doorways as possible. "What if it's the ferret?"

"It's not the ferret." Nicole shook her head.

"Why not? Kenneth said they're used to study the flu."

"*It's not the fucking ferret.*" Morpheus came closer, but Nicole shooed it away.

"Come on, Nicole. Think. It has to be something."

"Why? I didn't do anything. How do you know I'm not the control? How do you know I'm not just here to cause the rest of you to react in my presence? Maybe *I'm your* clue. I represent the virus, and the rest of you let it spread."

Kenneth was staring at her. "That's not logical. You said it yourself, Nicole. This started in your lab."

"Through no fault of mine."

"Come on now," said Miriam. "Nobody's *at fault.*"

But Deborah's expression said she wasn't convinced. "*Everyone's* at fault."

"Not me," said Kenneth.

"Nor me," Nicole added.

Deborah shook her head. "No. It doesn't fit. It's an experiment, and it looks like they followed a deliberate experimental design. I don't know much about the Enneagram, but I'm willing to roll with the theory that we represent the nine types — or that we're different enough to *be* different types, if not officially. There had to be other people you could say were 'at fault,' in some way, for the Phineas outbreak. Someone let it leave Nicole's lab and that person isn't here today. Tyler got something wrong with his CDC equations, but surely someone was supposed to double-check his work. But *that* person's not here, either."

Pacing, faster and with more purpose. "They chose us. Principals with a role in the outbreak, yes, but with none of our types overlapping. Nicole and Marcus were similar, but definitely not the same. Miriam, Zach was a little like you. Or even Ian, when he wasn't all riled up. But again, *different*. There must be a point, and we have to assume they knew what they were doing. The things they know about me, I barely knew about myself. If we want to understand this and maybe get out, we have to trust their judgment. Assume they got it right, by whatever standards they have. Then ask what they hope to get out of this. Because if this was about punishing us, we'd be dead already."

"Maybe they wanted to see if we'd infight. If we'd throw each other under the bus to save ourselves." Miriam saw Ian in her mind, shouting, throwing Nicole to what he'd thought was her death.

"Or if we'd confess," Kenneth said.

"But Marcus didn't say a thing," Nicole argued.

Kenneth tried again. "Admitting it to ourselves, maybe?"

"Shit," Deborah said.

"What?"

"Kenneth, your hospital ran short of supplies. You couldn't treat all the flu patients coming to you from Holiday Bend ... where Miriam enacted a curfew, and maybe where Patient Zero, with some unknown connection to Nicole's lab, lived."

"So what?" Kenneth replied.

"Why did you run short?"

"Shit happens. Too many patients."

"But you said you ran short of things like masks. You would have been in the first wave, since you were the epicenter. We would have been able to supply you with plenty. Only the staff and volunteers would need N-95s to protect them and prevent the spread. So the number of patients didn't matter."

"I guess we didn't order enough," said Kenneth.

"But how? You've had epidemic training. You know how many you need."

Kenneth's face changed. Miriam sat up, took notice. He looked like a man with an open cut, salted fingers brushing its surface.

"How many did you order?" Deborah asked.

"Forty."

"You mean forty-eight."

"Forty," Kenneth repeated. "My director joked that I ordered that many because it was her fortieth birthday that week."

"We sell them by the two-dozen."

"I had them break a box. Is that such a big deal?"

"Why?"

Kenneth seemed to resent it, saying nothing.

Deborah's head turned. Looked around. She settled on the swatches.

"Why paint chips?" Deborah asked Kenneth.

"What?"

"They gave Miriam a map of her quarantined town. That makes sense. They gave you paint samples. Why?"

"I don't know." But Kenneth looked like he was sitting on a tack.

"You said you had your hospital painted."

"Just one wing."

"Why?"

"Because it needed it. The place was falling apart."

"So?"

"I owe it to our patients to make them feel safe and comfortable."

Deborah was still churning, still digesting. "What time of year was that?"

"Why?"

"Just ... What time of year?"

"Over Thanksgiving break. The college was out, so I got a good crew. Fast and cheap."

"You run your fiscal year January to December? Or does it not follow a calendar year?"

"It's January to December. Wh—?"

"How did you pay for it?" Deborah cut him off.

Bullseye. Kenneth's eyes jumped like Mexican beans.

"End of the fiscal year," Deborah finished. "Maybe you're a lot better at budgeting than us, but we always run out of money by the end of the year. It's weird that you'd do renovations then. Especially if you had them break a box of N-95 masks, to buy forty instead of forty-eight. What happened — did you realize too late that you should have gotten more?"

"We had more volunteers than we expected. But like you said, by the end of the year, the budget was tight. And your masks are *expensive.*"

"Didn't the outbreak hit in December?"

Nicole and Miriam both nodded.

"It was unfortunate timing. We'd already spent money on painting."

"But don't you get a pandemic-prep stipend directly

from the government? That's usually the way our clients work. Separate budgets. It doesn't matter if you did your painting in November, as far as purchasing more masks was concerned."

Kenneth's face was hard. Mouth tight. Finally he blurted, "Fine. I borrowed from the pandemic budget to do the renovations. But it was the end of the year, right around Christmas. Spirits are always low in a hospital. I wanted to do what I could to make it better. It was only fair to the people who had to be sick over the holidays — only *right*. I didn't know a fucking *pandemic* was about to hit one town over! It was a one-month borrow. In January we'd have gotten a new budget and I'd have repaid what I took. It was dumb luck that ... that ..."

Miriam's hand went to her mouth. Nicole scooted away.

Deborah, curiously, seemed more fascinated than afraid.

A green light grew above Kenneth's head.

"Come on," Deborah said, half to Kenneth but half to herself. *"Feel it."*

There was a flash — green light lancing into his chest, making Kenneth glow, turning him to fire. He opened his mouth to scream, but then the rest of the pulse hit, and Kenneth was gone.

Acrid smoke. Tendrils of flame.

Accusation in her eyes, Nicole turned on Deborah.

"You goaded him into that. Damn you — *you did that on purpose!"*

Instead of answering Nicole's accusation, Deborah only faced them — first Nicole, then Miriam — and smiled.

"We ran out of masks, too," Deborah said. "Because instead of selling them to the Red Cross, who needed them most, I sold them to the highest bidders."

When the light hit this time, Miriam had to dive away to avoid its heat.

A green flash later, Deborah was gone as well.

And then there were two.

13

THE AIR SMELLED of ozone and Nicole was a mess, muttering, "Jesus. Jesus Christ."

Miriam stood. A grinding outside rent the world. More doors opened, more rooms vanished. Now they were ringed with arches filled with blackness. The world was a Möbius with no out. Leap through one door, come through another. Maybe that's why Deborah had done it — why she'd pulled her own pin, letting the aliens end her. The alternative, it seemed, was to stay here forever. If there'd been an exit, it was gone now.

There were no open doors left with rooms behind them. Only closed portals at each doorway, or nothingness.

The big clock made a final *chunk!* Then it stopped, its alien digits gone red.

"What's happening?"

"You tell me," Miriam said. "You're the three."

"We have to get out of here."

"How?'

"Pry open one of the remaining doors, while there's still time."

"I think time's up," Miriam said.

She looked at the silenced clock with its red glyphs. It no longer scared her. Same for the blackness. Suspense was the worst part of any horror — the waiting to see, and wondering what might happen. You could face the monster once you saw it.

The stopped clock.

The opening of more doors, underscoring their predicament.

The green beam was their only escape.

You entered a maze with eight other guilty parties. You argued. You had a realization. You died.

It was almost biblical. Before moving on, the soul was forced to stare into a mirror. To enter the afterlife with a clear conscience. If Miriam resented anything, it was that she felt force-fed. She'd never jibed with religion. Shame, after all that, to be judged by its standards.

Nicole was up. Around. Running from place to place as if the room might suddenly reveal itself as a mere contrivance.

"There's no point, Nicole."

"Fuck you," she said. "There's always a way."

"A way to win?"

"If you put it that way."

Miriam laughed.

"What?"

"It's so three of you."

"Oh, piss off, Miriam."

"What type, do you think, would go with the flow? Which of us would feel the undertow, then allow it to take us?"

"I don't know. You?"

Yes. Maybe me. A monster seen is better than one in the dark.

Miriam could wait to die or face it on her terms. Either way, she'd end up the same.

She looked at the bear.

Elyse had made that choice.

"I didn't do anything wrong," Nicole said, but not entirely to Miriam. She raised her face, shouted at the ceiling. "Do you hear me? I DIDN'T DO ANYTHING WRONG! I'M NOT SUPPOSED TO BE HERE!"

Her composure was gone. Her carefully cultivated air of casual exertion had already fallen apart. She'd had her hair in an *I-don't-give-a-shit* hiking ponytail that clearly gave a shit, and wore sneakers that tried to look practical while broadcasting cultivation and wealth. Now, the ponytail was coming undone, hair in a frazzle. A sneaker was untied, and her Yoga Bear hoodie was askew.

Miriam watched her, curiously detached. She looked at the clock, then out into the void. *I don't feel trapped anymore.*

Nicole was over by the cargo corner, grabbing ropes, tying them to beds, to anything she could. This time, instead of badgering others to risk themselves for her, she tied one around her own waist. The coil, between Nicole and the tie-off, was spaghetti on the ground beneath her.

"Hold the rope," she said, coming toward Miriam.

"No."

"Hold it!"

"There's no point, Nicole. I don't know what you did, but you're here for a reason."

The ferret chittered at her feet. Tried to climb Nicole's leg. She shoved it away and it came back, newly insistent.

"I'm not going to just give up." She went to one of the open doors, giving up on Miriam. "I'M NOT GOING TO JUST GIVE UP!"

With a final, vengeful look, Nicole tensed and lowered herself through the door.

She fell sideways out of the blackness, then spilled back into the room from the other side.

"Miriam? Help me."

But there was no help. This was mania. Twice more, Nicole jumped through doors only to fall back into the room from the other side. The rope still trailed her, advancing as she stretched it. The room itself had become a Cat's Cradle, threaded from doorway to doorway with rope that went nowhere.

"Miriam! Get up! HELP ME GET OUT OF HERE!"

Nicole was running for the door again when Miriam, in a sotto voice, said, "Nicole."

"What?"

"I sat on the quarantine. Delayed it, so my family could get out. I spread the flu. You may have made it, but I was the one who let it out of the bottle."

"Miriam? MIRIAM!"

But by the second time Nicole said her name, Miriam could already see the green glow surrounding her.

And beyond that, nothing.

14

Noise.

Miriam's eyes came open.

The room was different.

Or rather, it wasn't a room at all.

She didn't trust herself to sit up as she wasn't used to being dead and had in no way predicted Hell or Heaven would look like this. Even for Limbo, it was wrong.

Limbo was supposed to be all white light, floating forever with nothing to see, hear, or do. But this was a flat plain, moderately tall grass — the kind that might hold snakes.

The grass was trampled in front of her, and a rising hill with blue sky loomed beyond. A mouse trotted past her, squeaking. A single instrument in a grand symphony she'd heard often, yet had never appreciated the complexity of until this moment.

The sighing breeze and creaking of tree limbs, a chorus of birds both distant and near.

The mouse stopped, sat, stared right at her. Shouldn't it

run? But no, it was docile like a pet. All white, except where someone had spilled blue ink on it.

It squeaked. Ran a tiny albino paw over its muzzle. And then moved on, with better things to do.

"Miriam?"

At the sound of her name, she sat up. Fucking Nicole, meant to make even this place miserable.

But when Miriam turned, she saw it was Elyse.

"You're not dead," Miriam said.

"You, either." Elyse stooped to help her sit.

Her head was pounding, and her mouth was a desert. She had a six-keg hangover and her skin burned. She smelled of singed dust and hair. Above it all was the ozone tang of a high-voltage bug zapper.

"Move slowly. I know it hurts."

And it did. Miriam stopped when she was upright, with no urge to rise further.

"I don't mean to sound like a cliché, but ..."

"Where are we? Kentucky, apparently."

"Why Kentucky?"

"Why not?"

"I mean ..." She looked around.

"You mean how do I know?"

"I mean a lot of things." Foremost among them was the question of Elyse's mortality.

"A drink will help," Elyse said. "Can you stand?"

"I don't want to."

"You have to if you want a drink. They didn't give us a canteen."

"*They? Us?*"

"You found one?" came a male voice. "Who is that — Miriam?"

"Miriam," Elyse confirmed.

Miriam turned to see the speaker and it felt like someone jabbed several swords into her neck before peeling the skin away from her skull. She hoped Elyse's offer pertained to a figurative drink rather than a literal one. She wanted whiskey, not water.

When Miriam got her head around, she saw the speaker was Tyler, with his tidy little mustache. "Tyler?"

"Get her up," he said.

Together, Elyse and Tyler helped her to a stream threading the surrounding hills. She knelt, hesitated only a second, then made a bowl and drank from her hands. Relief was instant.

"Where the hell are we?" Miriam asked.

"Kentucky," said Tyler.

"Why does everyone keep saying 'Kentucky'?"

"Because we're in Kentucky," said Tyler, slipping a phone from his pocket. "My GPS started working again as soon as I got here."

"*How* did you get here?"

"Same as you. I teleported."

"*Teleported?*"

Tyler didn't have time to answer. Elyse had climbed to the crest of the hillside and waved her arms widely, and those she'd summoned were only just arriving. First Kenneth, then Marcus, Zach, and Deborah.

Ian brought up the rear, hesitantly. As her head cleared, Miriam thought she understood. If this is where you ended up after the green beam hit you, the newcomer could have been Nicole. Things between them were bound to be dicey, what with his trying to kill her and all.

"It was a test," Tyler said. "Like I told you."

"But ..." She looked around. Seven dead people around her, apparently back from their passing.

"Tyler figured it out first," Deborah explained. "I just put together what he'd already seen."

"You confess what you did ... and they *let you out?*"

"Apparently," said Deborah. "I knew I was taking a chance, of course, but I kept asking *why*. Like Tyler. They could abduct us from our homes. They could take us someplace where clocks and GPS didn't work — maybe a place where there *was* no time or space. But if they already knew our thoughts and still went to all that trouble, it didn't make sense that it'd be just to mess with us. The experts all say the Astrals are dispassionate. Torture, for torture's sake, just didn't seem ... well ... *logical*."

"They had to want something," Tyler said. "They put us there to find something out. Not what we'd done, but how we'd react to being *confronted* with our actions, or maybe how we'd react to what the others around us had done. They wanted to see how we tried to solve the puzzle."

"Tyler didn't know about the Enneagram, though," Deborah said. "We beat him on that one."

They were smiling around her, but Miriam could tell those smiles were only skin deep. There was an undercurrent of sorrow, despite how pleased the group was to have escaped.

Or maybe the mood was more sober. The emotion one feels when the pretty lies disappear and uncomfortable truths must be faced.

Miriam thought, *I delayed the quarantine. I killed millions of people who didn't have to die.*

But if there was any comfort, it was that she knew all of the others were thinking about their own faults.

Each of them had made a mistake.

Each had chosen something that suited them and cost

the world. It was a judge of character, like they'd said. And yes, they'd lived.

But now the blinders were off, and they'd live with guilt as their constant companion.

"Where's Nicole?" Zach said, starting to climb.

But Miriam thought she knew.

As the answer stood right now ... and probably into forever.

the world. It would be so strange, like they'd run. And you never found.

But, how the blacks worked and they'd tried with gold, father cover at first event.

"Would it, is it?" Sam laughed, like—

He stilled, disappointed, he—

the answer stood its own ... and probably that

15

HE SAT ON HIS HAUNCHES. Licking his parts, like he used to before the change. He could smell himself — his sense of smell was excellent. Always had been. It had to be, to live as he did.

He came through the bright light and into the wild. Into the grasslands, where the eight human survivors huddled, watching and waiting. They didn't see him. He stayed low. A ratter, meant to work in the darkness. It was nice here. Lots to investigate, many field mice to chase down and eat. But he had work to do. That had been the bargain. It was clear to him, after the change.

Morpheus sniffed the air, then went back through the ball of green light. A moment later he was under the desk in the shining metal room, all of them open now, the entire place threaded with rope from door to door. The work of an enormous spider.

In the middle, huddled, was the spider herself.

The one Morpheus had been asked, by the others, to watch.

So he lay down, watching. All he needed was eyes and

ears, he didn't need to understand. How could he? He was a ferret — even after they'd changed his mind, he knew that much. And most of the time, he could only be a ferret. He could sniff, he could chase, he could play curious and explore and climb and cavort — both in this place and in the meadow on the other side of the ball of green light.

Morpheus was free to come and go, the presence that joined his mind told him, so long as he did, indeed, come and go. His job, back when his original owner called him Fuzz, was simply "to be a ferret." Now, he had to be a watcher as well. He didn't need to understand what the woman with the rope around her waist was doing, or thought, or said to nobody left. The others could read his mind.

So Morpheus went closer to the one they called Nicole. Tried to lick her, as he'd done when they'd first arrived. She still didn't respond, still shoved him away. Why, if he was there for her? Why, if the others had been given inanimate object — a stuffed bear, a plastic kit with nothing inside, colors in a book, pictures on the wall — did the woman not appreciate that she'd been given something alive? Something that might, if she allowed it, be able to comfort her?

But Morpheus wasn't picky or needy. If Nicole chose to wallow, he was inclined to let her. She wasn't his companion. The world was his companion now. His owner was gone, in the ground the way of the pups he'd sired that hadn't made it.

Morpheus watched it happen. Saw his owner grow sicker and sicker, not returning to work, nor coming in for more doses of the disease he smelled on the man that day when he came back from the lab.

Back then, Morpheus didn't have any words and concepts for what was happening. He knew only that the man had something deadly and that Morpheus, as his pet, had gotten it, too. After the change — after the sky-things made him able to think — looking back had frightened him. His owner died, and Morpheus could have died, too. He didn't want more of the disease. He'd had it once. He'd run away after the man died in search of a place to pass on. He understood, in some sky-thing way, that Morpheus himself had maybe been more responsible for the bad disease than any of the people — the eight who'd escaped, or the one who remained.

He'd gotten the bug. Taken it to someone else even after the men in masks came to carry his owner's body away. The humans thought they'd stopped the problem where it started, but Morpheus was the vector that changed all their plans.

But all this was retrospect — in truth, beyond his ability to reason. Morpheus survived the disease. That's all that mattered. He'd lived in the wild for a long time after that, until the sky-things came. They'd found him, same as the people.

There hadn't been nine in the alien maze. Counting Morpheus, there were ten.

As an observer, he was immune. If he remained an observer, he'd stay that way. He didn't have fault to admit like the humans. So this was his penance. His service, to be in two places at once. To report back. To give the sky-things, as he moved between the normal places and their all-metal prison, a mind to read to see what was happening.

When the sky-things saw a certain emotion — a certain change — in a human, they removed them from the prison.

If the change never came, the human remained.

He could tell, now, that the woman with the ropes might stay forever.

"I didn't do anything," she said to nothing — to the room itself.

It wasn't true. She'd covered for the sick man who'd gone home from her lab, convincing herself she'd done the right thing despite the later lies — despite the deceit bred to cover her deceptions. But unlike the others, she couldn't see through her smokescreen.

The woman was liar and lied-to. Two people at once, a schism in her core.

"Please ... I'm innocent."

Through Morpheus's tiny ferret mind, the sky-things heard her.

And there, in the room, she remained.

The End

A QUICK FAVOR...

If you enjoyed this book, please take a moment to write a short review on your favorite online bookstore so other readers can enjoy it, too.

Thanks so much!
    Johnny

ABOUT THE AUTHOR

Johnny B. Truant is the bestselling author of *Fat Vampire*, adapted by SyFy as "Reginald the Vampire" starring Spider-Man's Jacob Batalon. His other books include *Pretty Killer, Pattern Black, Invasion, The Beam, Dead City,* and over 100 other titles across many genres.

Originally from Ohio, Johnny and his family now live in Austin, Texas, where he's finally surrounded by creative types as weird as he is. His website at JohnnyBTruant.com features his Creator Diary, additional works, fan extras, behind-the-scenes peeks, early access, and a whole lot more.

ALSO BY JOHNNY B. TRUANT

Robot Proletariat Series

En3my

Robot Proletariat

The Infinite Loop

The Hard Reset

Cascade Failure

Reboot

The Invasion Series

Longshot

Invasion

Contact

Colonization

Annihilation

Judgment

Extinction

Resurrection

The Tomorrow Gene Series

Null Identity

The Tomorrow Gene

The Tomorrow Clone

The Eden Experiment

Stand Alone Novels

Pretty Killer

Pattern Black

Burnout

The Target

The Island

Devil May Care